ℨ ℨ ℨ

The instant she laid eyes on Saul, her expression changed. It softened—or rather, it *melted*—right before my eyes. I wasn't sure what was happening, so I glanced over at him. He, too, had suddenly developed that dreamy look. The two of them just stared at each other for what seemed an eternity, with neither of them saying anything. The whole thing was a bit embarrassing, if you ask me.

"Hi, Rachel," I said, feeling obligated to break the unusual silence that seemed to have gripped everyone all of a sudden. "Uh, I'd like you to meet Saul, a friend of mine. Saul, this is Rachel."

Their eyes never left each other. "Hello, Rachel," Saul said. In his usual fashion, he shook her hand. But somehow, the crisp friendliness that generally accompanied that action was nowhere to be found. Instead, they sort of clung to each other.

CRAZY IN LOVE

Cynthia Blair

FAWCETT JUNIPER • NEW YORK

RLI: $\dfrac{\text{VL 6 \& up}}{\text{IL 7 \& up}}$

A Fawcett Juniper Book
Published by Ballantine Books
Copyright © 1988 by Cynthia Blair

Library of Congess Catalog Card Number: 87-92127

ISBN 0-449-70189-1

Manufactured in the United States of America

First Edition: August 1988

1

There may be no such place as never-never land, but there is a place called New York City, where all kinds of crazy things can happen. When I was growing up in Boston, during the first fifteen years of my life, I thought New York was just another city, like Cleveland or San Francisco or Dallas. But then my father's company offered him a promotion, and being the loyal corporate executive that he is, he eagerly followed golden opportunity, even though it meant dragging his family away from the place they'd always called home. After just a few short weeks I could see that I had been wrong about New York. My new school, the neighbors in the thirty-story building that my family moved into, even the people I passed on the street—well, it didn't take long for me to realize that New York is magic.

All that happened two years ago. A lot has transpired since the Spooner family made the big move away from its New England roots: I made some great new friends, went out on my first date, and decided that what I want most out of life is to become a songwriter. I began to think I'd become so cosmopolitan and sophisticated that nothing could faze me anymore. But then something so exciting, so beautiful, so absolutely *romantic*, happened that I decided that no matter how much living you do, no matter how much you're exposed to, there is always the possibility of witnessing something so unexpected that you go back to believing in Peter Pan and Santa Claus and the Tooth Fairy all over again.

I suppose it's important to mention right at the beginning that the eye-opening experience I'm referring to happened not to me, but to my very best friend in the whole wide world, Rachel Glass. Yes, I know. The first thing anyone ever notices about Rachel and me is the odd combination of our names. Rachel Glass and Sallie Spooner. We sound like characters in a children's book about kitchen utensils. Despite our last names, however, we have very few similarities. At least on the outside. Underneath it all, deep down where it really counts, Rachel and I are so much alike that I sometimes think that if there's such a thing as reincarnation, we must have been twins in another life.

As I said, though, we seem very different on the surface, and it took me a while to discover that Rachel and I had been cut from the same mold. When we first met each other, I didn't even like her. I was a junior in high school, and it's funny to think that if I hadn't twisted my ankle on the stairs of the subway station at Fifty-ninth Street and Lexington Avenue, I probably would never have come into contact with the girl who ended up becoming my blood sister.

Perhaps I should go back to the beginning. About a year ago, when I was just starting my junior year of high school, I had the bad fortune of falling down the stairs of the subway station on my way home from seeing the latest movie at the Coronet, one of the theaters right across the street from Bloomingdale's, with my younger sister, Jenny. It had been a wonderful day, one of those brisk, bustling Saturdays when the city had just started coming back to life after a dreary, stagnant summer. It must have been a couple of weeks after Labor Day, because school had just gotten going again.

Anyway, I was dragging Jenny down the steps of the station, my mind half caught up in the film I'd just seen and half obsessed with getting us both home on time. It was late, later than it should have been, because Jenny and I had gotten so involved in a record sale at Alexander's that we'd missed the two o'clock show and ended up waiting around for the four o'clock. Mom would be worried, I knew; she had never really adjusted to New York and still harbored constant fears that we would be kidnapped off the streets and smuggled away to South America or something. She truly is a New Englander at heart and always will be, I suppose.

All this may seem irrelevant, but it does prove that I had a good reason for being so distracted that I failed to notice that the set of steps I was running down continued on after stopping at a platform. I turned the corner, and the next thing I knew, I was sprawled across the concrete floor. It didn't take long for a small crowd to form. I don't know if those people were sympathetic, or if they were merely annoyed that someone's prostrate body was blocking their way.

At any rate, I was so embarrassed by the whole thing that I felt absolutely no pain until a little old man helped me to my feet with all the gallantry of an English nobleman. It was then that I blithely went ahead and forced all my weight upon my left foot, prepared to continue on my way with at least some remaining traces of dignity. Instead, I crumpled, falling to my knees in an equally dramatic and mortifying manner. If it hadn't been for Jenny's strong shoulder, I don't know how I ever would have gotten back up those stairs and into a taxi. For all I know, I might still be lying on the subway platform, an irritating obstruction to commuters who hurry toward the Number Six train or the pretzel stand a few feet away.

To make a long story short, it turned out that my accident was more frightening and more embarrassing than damaging. Once my mother recovered from her initial shock and stopped hurling those I-told-you-New-York-was-no-place-to-raise-two-teenage-girls looks at my father, she coaxed Dr. Brooks, the husband of one of her friends, into making an unprecedented Saturday-night house call. He poked around for a few minutes, ignoring my agonized expression, then concluded that it was nothing more than a mild sprain. Needless to say, I was relieved. The prospect of spending the first few weeks of school in a cast, hobbling around on crutches and developing shoulders like a football player, had been haunting me since I had sat back in the yellow Checker cab and assessed the situation.

Once I realized that there was no real harm done and that, according to Dr. Brooks, all I had to do was keep off my foot for a few days and then avoid strenuous exercise for a few weeks, I was able to enjoy my new role of invalid. Jenny did all kinds of nice things for me, things that she never would have tolerated otherwise. She would put a stack of my favorite records on the stereo in my bedroom, then return after a few hours to replace it. She trotted down to the bookstore the Monday after my fall to pick up some light reading for me, something that wouldn't tax my poor traumatized brain. She even offered to check in with my teachers to see what I would be missing during my brief vacation from school, but I quickly assured her that such a dramatic step wouldn't be necessary. There would be enough of that once things got back to normal, I knew, and there was no use hurrying the process.

Unfortunately nothing lasts forever, and it wasn't long before I was pronounced well enough to go back to school. The one stipulation, however, was that I avoid gym class for at least a month. This proved to be one of the most pleasing benefits of my ailing state, because I have never been particularly fond of anything requiring movement of any more than two muscles at a time. So while I pretended to be distraught for the sake of my gym teacher, Ms. Mead, I was secretly jubilant. The result of my new unathletic status, however, was that my entire schedule of classes was rearranged. I was transferred into a gym class that met during last period, so that I could go home earlier each day, supposedly to rest my foot. And that's how my chemistry class was changed from seventh period to first period.

My revised schedule required little real readjustment, because most of my teachers were the same as they had been under my original schedule. What was different was the group of kids in my classes. When I limped into my new chemistry class on my first day back at school, I found that I had been paired off with a lab partner I had never even heard of, much less met. All I knew about her was her name and the fact that she kept notes in a fabric-covered notebook in an extremely neat handwriting. She even went so far as to underline the important points with a red fountain pen! It was for this reason, trivial as it may seem, that I instantly took a dislike to Rachel Glass. Anyone who was that conscientious, I reasoned, could not possibly be my kind of person.

I suppose I was overreacting, but my distaste for my new lab partner made me very surly and tense. I imagined all kinds of terrible things about Rachel, especially that she was a snob and that she hated me because I was the "new kid" in the class and I limped and I still had a marked Boston accent that I couldn't seem to shake, no matter how hard I tried to imitate the other kids' way of talking. It was senseless, I know now, and I guess I even knew it then, but it was still very real. As I get older, I realize more and more that people don't always do the most reasonable thing. In fact, I'd say that much of the time they end up doing ridiculous things, for reasons that even they don't understand. And my behavior toward Rachel was the perfect example.

On the very first day of lab, Rachel and I stood hunched together over a Bunsen burner, trying to figure out how the stupid thing worked. I was mad at her, I guess because I figured that anyone who was so meticulous about keeping notes and making annotations in red ink should at least know how to do something as simple as light a Bunsen burner. Again, the fact that I was as lost as she was was completely irrelevant to me. All I did was scowl and sigh deeply, until Dan Meyer, who at the time seemed to me about the cutest boy who had ever walked the face of the earth, took pity on us and came over to show us how.

Of course, once we saw him do it, we felt kind of silly for not being able to figure out such a simple thing ourselves. I would have been ashamed had I not already resigned myself to the fact that, at heart, I was a creative person and a romantic to boot. Therefore, I had no need for such trivial knowledge as the kind that is handed down in chemistry classes. Rachel, too, was not particularly suited to the scientific life, I was soon to find out. She was talented in languages, and while she had had as much difficulty as I with the crisis of lighting a Bunsen burner, she, at least, could have followed a set of directions had they had been printed in Spanish, Russian, or Portuguese.

At the time it seemed as if nothing was going right. Here Dan Meyer was thinking that we were both complete imbeciles, I was cross over my lamentable situation, my ankle was throbbing, and we still hadn't gotten started on the actual task we had been assigned. We had to begin by boiling water, achieved simply enough by setting up a metal ring on a stand above the Bunsen burner and placing a Pyrex beaker filled with water over the flame. This, at least, my fellow chemist and I managed to do successfully.

Unfortunately patience has never been one of my virtues. When a full thirty seconds had passed and the water still refused to boil, I became frustrated and exclaimed, "This stupid thing isn't working. What's wrong with it?" and I reached for the beaker.

The yelp that followed could probably be heard over in New Jersey. It wasn't enough that I had a nonfunctional foot; now I had to add red fingers to the list of physical dysfunctions. But Rachel pulled me over to the sink even before the pain had started to register, and she thrust my hand under cold running water. Once again my face ended up turning red, redder than my burned fingers. As I looked over at Rachel, though, expecting her to condemn my thoughtlessness, she grinned and said ruefully, "Hot glass looks like cold glass, but doesn't feel the same, claim nine out of ten users."

I burst out laughing then, not only because I was relieved that the pointless tension I had created between us had finally vanished, but because I had just discovered that Rachel Glass possessed the most valuable attribute known to humankind. She had a sense of humor. I think it was then and there that she and I became best friends.

That very same day Rachel and I had lunch together. And then we met again at noon the next day, and the next, and just about every day after. We got to know each other giggling over tuna fish sandwiches and cartons of milk, gradually revealing little bits and pieces of ourselves, reinforcing over and over again our mutual belief that we had been destined to meet. With each anecdote, each confidence, each revelation of a special crush or a secret dream, we became closer and closer, until we ended up spending most of our free time together.

One of the things that made me trust Rachel very soon

after we first started talking to each other a lot was the fact that when I told her that I wanted to be a songwriter, she didn't laugh. She didn't even look startled. And she certainly didn't give me that lecture on "practical skills" and "making serious career choices" that most people, even friends my own age, are always giving me. It was as if she could sense how sacred it was to me, and how by even telling her, I was letting her in on something that was very special to me.

Her secret ambitions were a bit less outlandish, although she admitted that her math and science teachers rarely appreciated the fact that she was mainly interested in languages and had mastered more of them than most people her age. Maybe the fact that she, too, was bent on one particular thing was what made her encourage me so. She said she thought it was terrific that I wanted to be a songwriter and suggested that I find somebody to work with.

I had thought of that before, of course. As I sat in my bedroom for hours, strumming my guitar and trying to think of a rhyme that made sense or searching for the perfect chord, I had often wished for a collaborator. While I usually wrote both words and music, I had to admit that it was writing the lyrics that I was most interested in. My melodies sometimes sounded flat, and while my family and my friends insisted that they were the most beautiful melodies they had heard outside of the Beatles' compositions, I could tell that they needed something to spice them up. Sometimes I knew I could profit from an objective opinion, but the problem was, I just didn't know anyone who was good at writing music or the least bit interested in forming a musical team.

But once Rachel had suggested it, I started thinking about it more and more, and decided that I was definitely going to have to start looking for someone to work with. If nothing else, this person and I could develop a sort of mutual admiration society and encourage each other to keep plugging away, even when the whole thing seemed like a complete waste of time, as it so often did. It's not always easy to spend a Saturday night all alone in your room, trying to find a word that rhymes with "caring," after you've ruled out "sharing" as being too predictable.

So, right from the start, Rachel was a pal. She understood me, and she wanted what was best for me. I, in turn, wanted what was best for her, which was how I got so involved in this thing. I mean, it's pretty hard watching your very best friend when she's about to make a decision that you think is horribly wrong, isn't it? Some people might consider it butting in to other people's business, where you don't belong, but I consider it friendship.

Still, it is hard to take sides when you end up siding against your best friend. Fortunately the bonds that existed between Rachel and me were strong enough to withstand anything, it turned out. After all, once two people have lived through two semesters of chemistry labs together, it takes quite a lot to sever those bonds of common experience.

And to think it was a Bunsen burner that first brought Rachel and me together.

2

Even though I have never considered going to school one of youth's most entertaining pastimes, I always end up looking forward to September. By the time August rolls around, New York is deadly. In the summer the city is like a desert, with long stretches of hot sidewalks that look like sand. Everybody clears out, with the sole exception of the Spooner family, or so it seems. There's still a lot going on—concerts in Central Park, the air-conditioned movies, about eighteen billion street fairs and block parties—but everything feels so stagnant that it's easier just to sit around and wait for it all to be over.

The summer before my senior year of high school was especially bad. For the very first time Rachel's family went away for the entire month of August. Her father is a doctor—a dermatologist, as a matter of fact, a stroke of luck which is of no small significance during these trying pimple-prone years—so he can make his schedule flexible when he wants to. The Glass family usually spreads its vacations over the year, a week here and a week there, but for some reason, Dr. Glass suddenly got the idea of renting a house near the sea for half the summer. Rachel was ecstatic, needless to say. Not only did she get a terrific tan; she also perfected her breast stroke. Of course, she could only do it in salt water, which was of little use to our school swim team, because it only functions in water which is seventy-five percent chlorine.

While Rachel was combing seaweed out of her hair and flirting with cute blond lifeguards, I was busy being miserable. I moped around the apartment for the whole month. That is, when I wasn't working my tail off as a waitress at Peppermint Park. That's an ice cream parlor which I used to love, before I went to work there for the summer. Now, the mere thought of a Rocky Road parfait makes me gag. Anyway, even my sister Jenny gave up on trying to drag me places with her and her friends. So by the time September came around, I was thrilled to have my best friend back in town. Even the prospect of another whole year of exams and French grammar and gym class could not diminish my glee.

I remember the day that the Glass family rode back into the city, their car almost bursting with suitcases and boxes and plastic beach balls that had just about lost all their air. I barely recognized Rachel when she climbed out of the car carrying an empty cardboard bucket from Kentucky Fried Chicken in one hand and a copy of *Lady Chatterley's Lover* in the other. She had that dreamy look she often gets when she's been daydreaming or reading or thinking really hard. I figured it was Sir Clifford who was responsible this time. Anyway, she was very deeply suntanned, and she looked thinner. She wasn't actually any thinner, she told me later, but all those hours thrashing away in the waves had turned her into some kind of Body Beautiful. Also, her hair was shorter. Rachel has thick, wavy hair, such a dark shade of brown that it looks almost black. That is, until you get a glimpse of her in the sunlight and you get a chance to check out all those neat red highlights. It had been really long, but somewhere between New York and Virginia she had gotten it chopped to shoulder length. Her eyes are really dark brown, too, and her tan, combined with her coloring, made her look wonderful.

To top it all off, she was wearing this nifty outfit: sunshine-yellow terry cloth jogging shorts and a striped orange-and-yellow tank top. She was the picture of health. All of a sudden I felt pale and wan and sickly, like some unfortunate city kid who had been forced to spend the summer frolicking in the gushing waters of illegally opened fire hydrants. You know, like the ones in the posters soliciting contributions for the Fresh Air Fund. Not that I've ever had a tan in my whole life. Even when my family went to Florida eight years ago, everyone else turned a nice healthy, toasty brown without even trying. They all got tan just from hanging around the pool a couple of hours each day and walking through the parking lot from the air-conditioned rented car to the entrance of the wax museums. Not me. All I got was sunburned eyelids and six huge freckles, four on my nose and one on each forearm.

The critical factor here is the fact that I have red hair. Not red-auburn or red highlights, like Rachel. I'm talking bright orange-red. And freckles, lots of freckles, even when I haven't seen the sun for ages. I would have freckles all over my face (and, confidentially, all over my entire body) even if I had grown up in Siberia and only saw the sun for about two hours once a year. I am basically your fair-skinned, green-eyed redhead.

No one else in my family has that coloring, just me. I used to think I was adopted, until I found Grandma Spooner's diary in the attic of our old house in Boston and discovered that before her hair had turned white, it was blazing red, just like mine. After that I got to be kind of proud of it, as if I were carrying on some hallowed family tradition or something. That was when I decided to let it grow long and crazy, instead of keeping it short in the hopes that it would remain unobtrusive. Now, I wear it halfway down my back.

Still, even with my famous Spooner coloring, I was no match for the sleek, brown Rachel. By the time she spotted me, I had decided to start jogging every morning and to investigate those body makeups that made you look as if you just stepped off a plane from Palm Springs. Until someone touches your face and your tan comes off on their fingers, or however that stuff works.

All that was forgotten very quickly. My soul mate had returned! Rachel dropped her book and her chicken bucket, and we ran toward each other. And there, right on East Seventy-seventh Street, we hugged each other and screeched like wild banshees, oblivious of the passersby who looked at us as if we were strange or, worse yet, obnoxious teenagers.

"I'm so glad you're back!" I screamed. "You don't know how much I missed you!"

"Of course I do! I missed you, too!" Rachel answered. Then we screeched for a while longer. After a few minutes, once the novelty of our reunion had worn off, we were able to tone it down to mere hysterical giggles. Gee, it felt great, having Rachel back.

I think it was on that day that we vowed to make our last full school year together, before we went off to college, our very best year ever. We made a pact, nothing fancy, just a promise to continue being best friends and to try hard to have as much fun as we could.

A week later we were back in school. Nothing like a little reality to put you back in your place. It wouldn't be easy dedicating ourselves to the proposition that the purpose of senior year in high school is to have as many jollies as possible before being shipped off to college and having to maintain some semblance of mature, responsible adulthood.

Not when you had as many courses as there are school periods in a day. Rachel was up to her newly pierced ears in language courses, and I had decided to tackle advanced music theory. Not to mention all the usual requirements: English, history, and my all-time favorite, gym. Fortunately Rachel and I had both finished up our science requirement with our mutual fiasco in chemistry.

You know that feeling that suddenly creeps up on you when you're back in school in September? You're sitting in some class or walking down the hall, usually the very first week of classes, minding your own business, when all of a sudden this revelation comes to you. It's like a vision. There you are, *back in school*, and you're bored silly. Here you'd been thinking that going back to school meant seeing all your friends again, and getting new shoes, and hearing all kinds of interesting gossip. And then, whammo, it hits you. "Read *The Love Song of J. Alfred Prufrock* by Friday." "Vocabulary test next Wednesday." "Half your grade will be determined by this term paper. . . ." Ugh. It always hits me like a baseball in the stomach.

Even music theory wasn't pulling me out of my temporary slump. It was going to be *hard*. I was experiencing those back-to-school blues on that first Friday of school when the novelty and excitement had just worn off. I was standing in front of my locker trying to decide which heavy textbooks to lug home. And it hit me. I can remember that I let out a low moan, kind of like the noise cows make.

I had thought I was all alone, but it turned out that good old Dan Meyer was just about to turn the corner, after having stopped at the water fountain. My crush on Dan had worn off considerably since the year before, when I had been mooning over him in chemistry. But let's face facts: Dan Meyer is kind of the Bon Jovi of my high school, with his thick, dark hair and his incredible eyes. You don't get him out of your system that easily once you've melted before his baby-blue eyes. Still, to use a trite but never-theless descriptive phrase, I thought that Dan didn't even know I existed.

Well, apparently he did. "Hi ya, Sallie!" he said in that careless, offhand way he has perfected. I swear, he must practice in front of the mirror. "How'd your summer go?"

"Fine. Terrific." I slammed my locker shut, feeling guilty all of a sudden. It was as if I had a body hidden in there instead of my dull old textbooks with their brown grocery-bag covers. But that's the thing about Dan and his gorgeous blue eyes. No matter how confident you're feeling, no matter how much preparation you've had for your conversation with him, you always end up looking like you're posing for animal crackers in his presence. The cool, sophisticated side of Sallie Spooner didn't stand a chance.

"Great. I'm glad to hear it. Did you stay in the city?" I nodded like some kind of wooden dummy. I could feel myself turning red. Sometimes I think I'm the only woman alive in this day and age who still blushes. You'd think I had taken lessons from Scarlett O'Hara.

"Too bad. I was lucky. Spent a couple of months out at my brother's place in Colorado. Beautiful country out there."

"Terrific." It's funny. I'm someone who usually talks a million miles a minute, but Dan Meyer's presence had this peculiar effect on me. If it could have been packaged, my parents would have bought it by the ton.

"Hey, listen, Sal, I'm in kind of a hurry, but I wanted to ask you something."

Now, I'd like to interject here that there is probably nothing I hate more in this world than being called Sal. Call me buddy, call me girlie—anything but Sal. Whenever somebody calls me that, I feel as if I should instantly sprout hair in my armpits and change into an undershirt with giant holes in it. But because of what Dan said next, I quickly forgot my resentment.

"I thought if you weren't busy tomorrow afternoon, we could go roller-skating in the park."

I gulped. Noticeably. I had had absolutely no time to prepare for that one. He just threw it out at me from nowhere. I turned redder; I'm sure of it.

"Sure. Sounds terrific." Whenever I'm nervous, I use the word "terrific" constantly. Every second word I use is "terrific." Then I remembered. "Oh, wait a second. I'm supposed to spend tomorrow afternoon with Rachel."

"Well, then, bring her along. And I'll bring my friend Fred."

"Fred? Who's Fred?"

"You know, Fred Abrams? He's one of my best friends. Surely you know Fred."

"Oh, yeah. Fred. Terrific." Terrific, again. There must be some weird correlation between my pulse rate and my compulsion to use that stupid word.

Anyway, within five minutes of that encounter, I had found a pay phone and left a message with Rachel's mother that she was to call me the instant she got home from school. My first date of the school year, and with Dan Meyer, no less! And, of course, Rachel's first date of the year, too. I wasn't sure what she thought about Fred Abrams, and I didn't know how she'd feel about having been set up with him without even knowing about it.

I suppose I should mention at this point that Rachel is Jewish. The reason I'm bringing that up now is that she mainly goes out with Jewish guys, people she knows from school or from temple. Or every once in a while her parents come up with some guy they want her to go out with. The Glass family is not what I'd call religious, but they do have a very strong sense of their Jewish heritage. Her mother preserves as many of the traditions as she can, and she's passed along an appreciation of both the heritage and the traditions to all her children. So Rachel tends to be selective about the boys she goes out with.

Fred Abrams also happened to be Jewish, a fact that I pointed out to her later on that afternoon when I ended up arguing with her on the telephone.

"But you've always liked Fred!" I insisted, desperately afraid that the plans for our double date would get screwed up. "You haven't once, in the whole time I've known you, said one word against Fred Abrams."

"Sallie! I don't think I've ever said a single word, for *or* against, Fred Abrams. I don't even *know* him! And now you've got us set up in this cozy little foursome."

"But maybe you'll turn out to like him. Can't you look at this as a rare opportunity to get to know somebody better? Even make a new friend? You know what they say—'Make new friends, but keep the o-old. . . .'"

"Don't sing, Sallie. Not now, when you're using me as a way to get to Dan Meyer."

"Isn't that a bit exaggerated? Few people would call me an opportunist, under these circumstances. Look, Fred's a lovely guy. He's smart, he has a good sense of humor. . . ."

"Right. And he's a nice Jewish boy. You sound just like my Aunt Libby, our family's resident matchmaker."

"It's only roller-skating. And it's only for a few hours. And I'll be there. You can always talk to me if all else fails. Besides, it might even turn out to be fun. You and Fred could end up becoming a hot item."

"Humph." Rachel sighed, but I could tell she was about to give in. "We-ell, okay. But only because you're my best friend. Keep in mind that I wouldn't do this for anybody else but you."

"You're a peach!"

By the time the next afternoon rolled around, I had

washed and blow-dried my hair, tried in vain to cover some
of my freckles with Bonne Belle liquid foundation, and
changed my clothes at least five times. My excitement
turned to nervousness as I strolled over to Rachel's house,
the rendezvous point for all four of us before our trek over
to Central Park together. It's not that I generally worry about
going out with guys; it's just that I had had this ridiculous
crush on Dan Meyer for such a long time that I'd built him
up to be a real superman in my mind. So I naturally felt that
I could be nothing short of superwoman myself.

When I got to Rachel's apartment, I started to feel a little
more like a normal person and less like someone who was
about to appear before the grand jury. Rachel's attitude was
hardly one of excitement, much less anxiety. In fact, the
looks she kept giving me made it clear that she was only
going through with this whole thing for my sake.

"I'll go," the look in her blazing dark eyes said, "but
don't expect me to have a good time. And don't expect me
to forget this favor, either."

Still, she was making as much of an effort as I was. She
was dressed in acid-washed jeans and an "I Love New
York" T-shirt, and I could tell that she had spent a lot of
time getting her hair just right and putting on her mascara
and blush very carefully, just as I had. I started feeling
pretty good. I knew that I looked as nice as I could, and I
was wearing my favorite new outfit: lavender pinwale
corduroy overalls and a pale purple-and-pink plaid blouse. I
had even worn matching lavender plastic combs to keep my
hair out of my face.

Dan and Fred showed up at the Glasses' front door before
Rachel and I had a chance to talk. But I could tell by the
way she was acting that she was starting to get into it. Fred
Abrams is not a bad-looking guy, and he's got a great sense
of humor. He also has a brain, which is more than I can say
for most of the guys we go to school with. Rachel started

flirting with him as soon as we started walking over to the park, and I relaxed.

At least I relaxed as far as the Rachel-and-Fred duo was concerned. As for Dan, I still felt as if I had to try really hard, as if I had to impress him. I ended up doing what I usually do in a situation like that: clamming up. Rather than saying something stupid, I always opt for saying nothing at all. It's amazing how many guys have actually said, after a first date, "Gee, Sallie's a nice girl, but she's awfully *quiet*, isn't she?" Me! Old blabbermouth herself! It just goes to show you what nerves can do.

I found myself lapsing into my typical first-date silence, even when we stopped at the roller skate store on Lexington Avenue to rent skates for the afternoon. Dan didn't seem to notice, though. He talked constantly. He didn't stop once, not even when we started to cross Park Avenue without checking the street lights and nearly got run over by a taxi. As the taxi driver yelled at us out the window in some indiscernible language, Dan kept on talking.

What he talked about was himself. He told me about his family, his basketball team, the Whitney Houston concert he'd gone to the week before at Madison Square Garden, the reason why he couldn't wear wool sweaters, and about a dozen other topics of interest to no one else except his mother and possibly his shrink, if he had one. But I was trying to be a good listener, so I just smiled and nodded a lot. I guess I was even grateful that I wasn't being called upon to make any social contribution.

Meanwhile, it seemed as if Rachel and Fred were really hitting it off. They, too, were chattering away. Rachel had stopped giving me those dirty looks, so I figured I was back in her good graces again. We strolled into the park, found a bench, and laced up our skates. Now, as I have already mentioned, athletic prowess has never been one of my strong points. I can stand up on skates, and I can get around okay on flat surfaces, but give me a hill—going up *or* down—and it's all over. Rachel is a bit better than I am, but she's no Dorothy Hamill, either. As we all got ready to start skating, Rachel and I glanced at each other ruefully. I began to wonder if we should have insisted upon doing something a bit more sedentary, like going to the movies or sitting on a curb somewhere. But the die was cast.

"Come on, Sal," Dan called as he stood up with ease and assurance. I thought he would reach for my hand and expect to glide off with me in the tradition of Fred Astaire and Ginger Rogers, and I blanched. But instead, he took off and called to me, "I'll race you!"

"Hey, wait up!" A few seconds later, Fred had taken off after him like a bolt of lightning.

Rachel and I sat on the bench, staring at our knees. I distractedly ran my fingernails against the lavender corduroy of my overalls. I love that feeling of running your nails over the little ridges. It was a good thing, too, since it suddenly looked as if there was a strong possibility that I'd spend the rest of the afternoon doing exactly that.

"Was it something I said?" Rachel joked, and we both burst out laughing.

"And to think I was worried about my grace and form!" I exclaimed. "Come on, let's trip the light fantastic." I stood up cautiously, then reached for Rachel's hand. "We'll probably have a better time without them, anyway."

The two of us gingerly made our way down one of the roads that run through Central Park. On the weekends when the weather is good, the roads are closed to traffic. So all we had to contend with was bicycles, skaters with earphones who looked as if they'd just stepped off the roller-disco floor, and an occasional dog who, for some unknown reason, had taken it upon himself to discourage skating in Central Park by barking and jumping up on innocents like ourselves.

"You realize we might never see them again," I said after about an hour of us wheeling around the park in slow motion, clutching at each other and occasionally dragging each other down to the hot, grainy pavement.

"No such luck. Here come Rough and Ready now."

Sure enough. Dan and Fred came racing toward us. Instead of looking apologetic, though, they looked cross.

"Hey, what happened to you girls?" Dan demanded. "We kept waiting for you to catch up."

I was tempted to explain that we had been discovered by a famous film director who had insisted upon filming our agile movements for his latest picture, but I stopped myself. Often my wonderful cynical humor is wasted on people who are too dense to understand it.

Instead, I turned to him, and still holding on to Rachel to keep myself from spilling to the ground in an undignified heap of lavender corduroy and spinning wheels, I growled, "What happened to *us*? What happened to *you*? Why didn't you wait, or come looking for us?"

I am generally a pretty easygoing sort of person, and it is not in my nature to make waves. So once I had voiced my discontent, I made sure things returned to an even keel pretty fast. Within a minute or two, we were all friends again. Just a happy foursome, tripping through Central Park on a sunny Saturday in Indian summer.

"How about getting a Coke somewhere?" Rachel suggested. "I'm dying of thirst." I had to admit that she looked a little flushed. Personally, I was completely drained from the experience of fighting gravity for over an hour, all in the name of appearing to be a trendy, fun-loving New Yorker.

We found our old bench and changed back into our shoes. My feet had never been so happy before in their whole lives. Solid ground had never felt better.

"Where shall we go?" Now that I was stable again, it was easy to return to my usual chirpy self.

"There's a coffee shop on Madison," Fred informed us. "Let's go there."

Spirits were high again, or at least optimistic, as we scrambled into a red leatherette booth at a tiny coffee shop named after one of the Greek islands. When the waiter came by, Dan said in a very authoritative voice, "I think we all know what we want. Sal?"

Rachel and I ordered Diet Cokes. I really felt like a glass of milk, but while I'm pretty secure for a seventeen-year-old, I'm not quite secure enough to order milk on a first date.

"And my friend here and I will have a couple of beers."

Rachel and I exchanged glances again, the kind that say more than mere words ever could.

"You guys got ID?" the waiter asked.

The legal age for ordering beer in a restaurant in New York is twenty-one. I knew for a fact that both Dan and Fred were seventeen, because that had been one of the many fascinating facts Dan had thrown at me while we were walking across town to the park. I braced myself for a scene.

"Hey, who do you think you are?" Dan said, trying to sound mean. Instead, he sounded so defensive that he looked ridiculous. "I'm twenty-one, and so is my buddy here." He looked to Fred for support.

"That's right," Fred chimed in. "We're twenty-one."

"I need to see your ID," the waiter went on. I thought he was being extremely patient.

"Let me see the manager," Dan insisted. At that point I felt like grabbing Rachel and fleeing, just sliding back into our rented roller skates and rolling away into anonymity. She, in turn, had that look on her face that is halfway between helpless and disgusted.

"The manager isn't here right now. Look, why don't you guys just order something else?"

Oh, no, that would have been too easy. I could see by the look on Dan's face that he had no intention of complying with such a reasonable request. Fred, too, was glowering at the poor waiter. It was at that point that I decided to buck Amy Vanderbilt's code of good etiquette. I stood up and said in as calm a voice as I could manage, "This is stupid. I'm leaving. Come on, Rachel." I flounced out of the coffee shop, leaving Dan, Fred, and the waiter openmouthed. I could hear Rachel behind me, or rather I could hear her wheels spinning in midair as she hurried out after me.

"Rachel," I fumed, once we were out on the street, "was I being unreasonable? Would you say that I'm an impetuous person, prone to unjustified behavior?"

"Not at all." She, too, was furious. We marched across town toward the skate-rental place, our faces twisted into angry frowns. Then, all of a sudden, as if on cue, we looked at each other, then dissolved into peals of laughter.

"Oh, Sallie!" Rachel cried. "I couldn't believe that whole scene! I felt like I was *baby-sitting* those guys, not going out with them!"

"I know! If I had realized what a turkey Dan Meyer is, I never would have agreed to go out with him!"

"You know, this isn't really very funny," Rachel said, once we had calmed down and were breathing normally again. "Actually, it's pretty sad. I mean, this is what we have to look forward to: a full year of going out with total turkeys."

"You're right." It was a sobering thought, and by the time we had returned our skates and strolled over to Rachel's apartment, we were down in the doldrums.

"What's wrong with these guys?" Rachel wailed as we went into her kitchen to fortify ourselves after that whole ordeal.

"What are you two moping about?" Rachel's mother, who happens to be one of my very favorite people in the whole world, and the woman that I consider to be my second mother, came into the kitchen and sat down at the table with me. "Didn't you have a good time on your double date?"

Rachel and I both cast her looks of utter disgust.

"Fun?" Rachel squealed. "I would have had a great time if it had been just me and Sallie. But those guys ended up ruining the entire afternoon."

"It's true," I agreed. "We ended up skating together, just me and Rachel, because we weren't up to chasing after two wild men on wheels. And then they insisted upon giving the waiter at the coffee shop a hard time because they ordered beer and then couldn't prove they were twenty-one."

"*Are* they twenty-one?" Mrs. Glass asked.

"Of course not! I think they're about nine."

"It's terribly discouraging," I concluded. "This does not bode well for our futures as *femmes fatales*. Why are boys like that?" I gratefully accepted the glass of cold milk that Rachel handed to me.

"I can remember feeling the same way when I was in high school," Mrs. Glass said. "It takes most boys longer to mature. I guess these two just haven't caught up with the girls their age yet."

"*Most* boys! They're *all* like that, or so it seems." Rachel was emphatic. "Right now I feel like putting myself on 'hold' until next year, when I get to college. Who needs to cater to these numbskulls?"

"It was a wasted afternoon." I felt responsible, too, because I was the one who had been swept off my feet by Dan Meyer's lustrous locks and baby-blue eyes. "Shall we take a vow of celibacy?"

"At least temporarily." Rachel sighed, then took a sip of milk. A little liquid refreshment was making the world look a bit better, but it had nevertheless been a discouraging afternoon.

"Hey, come on, you two," Mrs. Glass urged. "You'll meet some worthwhile boys one of these days. It just takes time, that's all. Surely you've both seen that T-shirt that says, 'You've got to kiss a lot of toads before you finally find the prince.'"

"Well, considering all the toads I've put up with over the past few years," I lamented, "I'd say I'm about due for a prince."

"Me, too," Rachel agreed. "In the meantime, however, we do have each other. Why don't you say we save the rest of this afternoon? Let's go see that new movie. You know, the one with Jane Fonda in it."

"But it's such a lovely day!" Mrs. Glass protested. "Do you want to spend it holed up inside a dark movie theater?"

"I'd say we've both had enough fresh air for one day. Let's hear it for chairs and the enjoyable pastime of sitting." I groaned, massaging the backs of my calves. I could already feel those muscles stiffening up, screaming at me, "Sallie, what have you done? We thought you were on our side!"

"I don't blame you for being disappointed," Mrs. Glass said as she stood up and pushed her chair to the kitchen table. "But I promise you that things will change. There will be Prince Charmings, or at least reasonable facsimiles, in your futures."

At that point all I could do was hope that Mrs. Glass, being older and wiser, was correct in her prediction. But in the meantime, I looked forward to spending the remainder of the afternoon enjoying the companionship of another female.

"Let's get moving," I said, starting to look forward to the movie. "Jane Fonda awaits us." Arm in arm, Rachel and I marched out of the kitchen.

3

It was almost entirely by accident that I first became interested in songwriting. One night, when I was still living in Boston, I was baby-sitting for some friends of my parents, the Clarkes. I remember that I was supposed to be studying for a math test the next day. Logarithms are not exactly the most exciting thing in the world, however, and after a couple of hours of staring at those log charts with thousands of numbers on them and doing all those dull practice problems, I decided to chuck the whole thing, at least for a little while.

I turned on the television set and started switching from station to station, looking for something that would be more interesting than "log 387." That shouldn't be too difficult, I know, but all I could find was news shows. I had something a bit more entertaining in mind than weather reports and film clips of diplomats shaking hands with each other. So, eventually I stumbled upon the Public Broadcasting station—you know, educational TV. And there was this man teaching guitar.

From what I can recall, the guy was a bit lacking in the

personality department. But one thing was for sure: he made it look as if playing the guitar was as easy as . . . well, easier than doing logarithms. I quickly cased the Clarkes' living room, but not surprisingly, there were no guitars around. But there was a tennis racket in the hall closet, thrown in among the rubber boots and delinquent hangers that had fallen off the rod.

The tennis racket was warped and frayed, and I don't think it would have been much good on the courts. But it made a perfect guitar. I remained glued to the set for the next twenty minutes or so, the fingers of my left hand wrapped around the handle uncomfortably as I copied the man on the TV screen, my right hand strumming the strings of the racket. I guess it would have looked sort of weird if anyone had wandered in, but the kids I was baby-sitting were busy tying each other up, or whatever it was they were doing up in their room.

I kept on watching that show, every week for the next month. I had to leave behind the Clarkes' makeshift guitar, but tennis rackets seem to be one of those things that families always have lurking in some closet somewhere. They're like safety pins and bobby pins: you never actually *buy* any, but somehow they're always around when you need them. So I found an old tennis racket up in the attic, in the same trunk where I had found my redheaded grand-mother's diary, and starting strumming away.

I guess I did look pretty pathetic. I didn't realize that anyone was even aware of what I was doing, but mothers have eyes in the backs of their heads. On my birthday Mom presented me with a huge, bulky gift—and sure enough, it was a guitar. A *real* guitar, one that made sounds and could not be used at Wimbledon for anything other than music to applaud by.

I think I progressed more rapidly on the guitar than I had on the tennis racket, although it's impossible to tell. Not only did I religiously attend my weekly lessons with the television screen; I bought myself a book of songs with little charts to show the chords that went with them, and started to learn to play actual music. The very first song I ever played from start to finish was "The Streets of Laredo." Now that's a song you don't hear too much anymore, outside of rodeos and camp fires on the cattle range, and I rarely get requests for it. But for me it was a milestone, and true inspiration. I could play real music!

The funny thing about playing the guitar is that writing your own songs seems almost inevitable. Once you start teaching yourself to play the stuff you've heard on the radio and your record albums, you realize that most songs are made up of only three or four chords. And the same three or four chords, at that. That's an earth-shattering discovery, for once you've made it, you start putting together little tunes without even trying very hard.

I tend to go overboard on things, and I became obsessed with music. Little melodies would occur to me at the most unlikely times—while getting out of the shower, talking on the phone, even trying to fall asleep at night—and I would hop out of the bed or the bathroom or wherever I happened to be and jot them down on the back of a grocery receipt or whatever I could find. And then, when it was more convenient, I would sit down and try to fit words to the melody, and then find on the guitar the chords that I could already hear in my head.

It wasn't long before the fame bug hit me. Spending a lot of time banging out tunes plants wild ideas in your head. I saw stardom, I saw fortune . . . most of all, I saw the thrill of having talented, well-known performers recording songs I had written. Sallie Spooner, Incorporated. While my friends were daydreaming about becoming doctors and lawyers or running away to the south of France with Rob

Lowe, I was trying to picture my name on the label of a record as it went round and round on the turntable.

The problem was that I had no idea of how songwriters actually got their songs produced. That put a real damper on my plan. So I decided to sit it out until golden opportunity came knocking at my door. I didn't know how or when it would, but somehow I had faith that eventually it would all work out. In the meantime I kept plugging away, churning out song after song. I ended up being the hit of many a party, that's for sure.

"All things come to her who waits." Isn't that a famous expression? In my case it proved to be true. About a week after my less-than-memorable afternoon with Dan Meyer and friends, I was sitting in my room, puttering around and half listening to the radio. It's amazing how much time I spend doing that. I pretend I'm keeping up with music trends, but really I'm just lazy a lot of the time.

Anyway, all of a sudden the disc jockey made this announcement that made my ears perk up like a dog's. He said that the station, one of the largest in New York, was holding a songwriting contest for high school kids living in the city. All you had to do was call this number for more information. . . . I quickly wrote the telephone number down on a scrap of paper. Two seconds later I was dialing it.

The woman who answered the phone sounded nasal and bored, not at all aware of the excitement that that announcement was causing. She explained in a monotone that the contest had two levels. First, one songwriter would be selected from each competing high school in the city. Second, out of those entrants, one would win the citywide competition. Each person or group could only enter one song. The prize was phenomenal: the best song would be recorded by some still-unnamed but well-known rock group.

I tried to keep the hysteria out of my voice as I gave the

woman my name and address so she could send me an application. I was ecstatic! At last, opportunity had come knocking at my door! And they say you can't get rich and famous just staying at home in your room.

I spent the next hour howling and squealing, to my family, on the telephone to Rachel, and to just about everybody else I could think of to call. But then came the grim reality. None of the songs I had already written were deemed good enough for this competition. I had to come up with something that was so terrific, so *inspired*, that it couldn't lose. Not when the stakes were so high!

At the risk of sounding like a temperamental, complaining artist, I must say the next few days were hell. Inspiration simply would not come. The only melodies that drifted into my mind were those that were already famous. I tried listening to all my old records; I tried sitting in complete silence. I even tried sitting in a room that was completely silent *and* pitch black. It just wouldn't come, and I was rapidly becoming miserable.

So when my friend Sharon Burke called to invite me to a party the following Friday night, I was relieved. It was a welcome interruption, one that meant that for at least a few hours, I could quit agonizing over chords and notes that simply refused to fit together in any interesting fashion. As is the case with just about everything that happens to me, I called Rachel right after Sharon's phone call to see if she was going.

"Rach? It's me. Guess who just called."

"Don't tell me. Sharon Burke."

"Are you psychic or something?"

"No. You know how compulsive and organized Sharon is. I think she called all her friends in alphabetical order."

"You going?"

"Nope. I can't. Next weekend is a Jewish holiday. Yom Kippur."

I felt a slight twinge of panic. I'm so used to going everywhere with Rachel that sometimes I forget that I'm quite capable of handling social obligations on my own. Especially since Sharon is not exactly a close friend. We travel in somewhat different circles, and her parties are always full of people I don't know. I can find that either challenging or intimidating, depending upon my mood. I must have been in a reclusive mood, probably because I was turning into a wild, crazed songwriter who was tearing her hair out and never leaving her room and guitar except when forced to by parents or the New York State Board of Education.

"I'll miss you," I said. "You usually provide me with moral support at Sharon's parties."

"You'll handle it," Rachel assured me. "Trust me."

By Friday evening the prospect of a party had become a welcome one. I enjoyed going through the routine of getting ready to go out. Jenny was hanging around, watching me enviously, which made me feel big sisterish and very important. She's a good kid, Jenny is, even when she's not feeding my ego by looking up to me.

"Where are you going tonight?" She had wandered into my room and plopped down on the bed on her stomach, her chin resting in her hands. "Got a hot date?"

"No. I'm sworn off men, for a while. Remember? That wretched afternoon with Dan Meyer had left me with a lingering case of the heebie-jeebies." I stood before my closet, trying to decide which blouse to wear with my powder-blue corduroy jeans. I was really into corduroy that September.

"So where *are* you going?"

"To a party."

"Who's giving it? Anyone I know?"

"Jenny, do you like the blouse with the blue flowers, or this one with the little trucks?"

"Trucks. Who's giving it?"

"Sharon. Do you know her?"

She made a face. "Isn't she the one with the squirrel cheeks?"

"Jenny! Sharon happens to be a lovely girl."

"Maybe, but she reminds me of a squirrel." She was right. Sharon does look kind of like the personification of some Walt Disney character.

"Are you sure about this shirt?" I asked her. "I think it has too much purple in it."

"Nonsense. You're being too critical. Blue and purple look great together. Besides, you're an artist, and you're supposed to dress weird. Your fans will be disappointed if you don't."

"Hah! Fans? I can't even write one stupid song for that WROX contest."

"Still no luck, huh?" Jenny sighed. I appreciated her sympathy. For someone so young, she has a tremendous understanding of the trials and tribulations of pursuing art. "Maybe you need a partner."

"Surely you're not offering . . ."

"No, not me. You know I'm tone-deaf. I mean someone musical."

"Easier said than done. I've been through all this before." I peered into the mirror to see if I had put my tea rose blush on right. It needed more blending. "Should I wear combs tonight or go natural?"

"Let me see." Jenny considered both options as I presented each one to her. "*With* combs. The blue makes your eyes look greener."

That made no sense to me at all, but I didn't argue. I really do trust Jenny's judgment. She may be tone-deaf, but she has a great eye for color. I wouldn't be surprised if she ends up becoming a famous painter one day.

"Anyway," I went on, "it's not easy to form a partnership. You have to find someone you can work with without fighting all the time, as well as somebody who's into the same style of music you are."

"But look at Rodgers and Hammerstein! Lennon and McCartney! Steve and Edie!"

"Cute. But for now, I'm afraid I'll have to seek fame and fortune on my own." I kissed her on the cheek before dashing out. "Have faith in me. I'll come up with a song that'll knock your socks off!"

"Oh, Sallie!" she yelled after me. "*Nobody* uses that expression anymore!"

Just as I had expected, Sharon's living room was packed with people, most of whom I'd never seen before. There were a few familiar faces, and ordinarily I would have gravitated toward the tried-and-true. Unfortunately the faces I recognized belonged to people who were not exactly my favorites.

"Great," I muttered under my breath as I made my way through the crowd, searching for someone to talk to. "Where is Rachel when I need her most?"

For a while I talked to Sharon, clinging to her desperately as if she were my best friend in the whole world. But then she ran off to retrieve another bag of nacho chips from the kitchen, and I found myself stranded once again. I leaned against the wall, trying to blend in with the wallpaper as I scanned the crowd, a stiff smile on my face. I turned my attention toward a bowl of pretzels that was nearby, studying each pretzel before I ate it. Anyone who noticed me probably thought I was checking for bugs.

It was then that I started thinking about resorting to Plan B, the unexpected-illness plan. It was simple: All I would have to do to escape from this uncomfortable situation was find Sharon and tell her about the sudden headache that had fallen upon me from nowhere. Probably all the excitement of her party, I could say. Still, I hated to do that, because I had only been hanging out on the sidelines of her living room for about ten minutes.

I continued leaning against the wall, and at one point I turned my head to feign interest in the couple who had started dancing over by the dining room table. You know how sometimes you can hear things through the wall that you can't hear through the air? Like when in old cowboy-and-Indian movies, the scout always puts his ear to the ground to see if he can hear horses coming from far away? Well, leaning my ear against that wall had the same effect. Through the noise of the voices and the clinking glasses and the music from the stereo, I could hear the soft strumming of a guitar.

It was intriguing, and of course, I was looking for anything that would absorb my attention, at least for a while longer until I could use my unexpected-illness plan. I used the mysterious sound of music as an excuse to disappear from the living room. I followed the hallway of the Burkes' apartment until I found a door that was ajar.

I stuck my head in. And there, sitting on Sharon's bed, was a guy I had never seen before, strumming a guitar. When he saw me, he stopped and got this really guilty look on his face. I got the feeling he was doing exactly what I was doing: hiding.

"Don't stop," I urged, going in and sitting down on the floor. "Pretend I'm not here."

He just nodded, and he started playing an instrumental version of "Here Comes the Sun." It was fantastic! I was amazed at how well he could play. My strumming and cautious picking was fourth-rate compared to the stuff he was doing. I was impressed, right from the start. Also, I couldn't help noticing that this guy was pretty good-looking. He looked kind of like Cat Stevens: black curly hair, worn shaggy and long; almost-black piercing eyes; a dark mustache and a beard. He was heavyset, although it was hard to see very much of him through his baggy jeans and plaid flannel shirt. He reminded me of a teddy bear. All in all, he was not what I had expected to find in Sharon Burke's bedroom.

"That's great!" I said when he had finished. "Boy, you really put my guitar playing to shame!"

"Oh, do you play?" he asked.

"Just a little." I suddenly felt very modest and very shy.

"Here. Let's see." He offered me his guitar and looked at me expectantly.

"Well, uh, maybe I should get back to Sharon's party." Now I generally jump at the chance to play for people. In fact, my friends sometimes have to beg me to stop. But this guy—well, he played like no one else I had ever heard, at least up close, and I had no intention of disgracing myself in front of him.

"Do you really want to do that?" He looked at me as if he couldn't understand why anybody would want to go back out there. I could tell that he certainly didn't.

"I guess not. But I can't play very well."

"Oh, come on. Try. After all, I played for you."

"Well, okay." I gingerly accepted the guitar. "What would you like to hear?"

"What do you like to play?"

"To tell the truth," I apologized, "I mostly play things I've written myself."

"Then play me something you've written."

By then I was really having heart palpitations. Not only was my guitar playing going to be put on the line, but my abilities as a songwriter as well. And I must admit that those piercing dark eyes were complicating things even further. I have always been a sucker for beautiful eyes.

But I mustered up all my courage and launched into one of the best songs I've written. It never misses, because it has a catchy beat and a pretty memorable melody. My voice cracked a few times at the beginning, but then, as usual, I got so into it that I forgot that anybody else was in the room.

When I was done, I glanced up. I could feel myself blushing.

"You wrote that?" he asked.

I nodded.

"It's great! I love it! Sing more!"

Without going into all the boring details, let me just summarize the next two hours by saying that I ended up playing every song I had ever written. I was even tempted to give my rendition of "The Streets of Laredo"; that's what a good listener this guy was.

And then he took his guitar back and sang some songs he had written. I was flabbergasted. His songs were wonderful! In fact, I had to keep asking him, "Did you write that, or is it from some record album?"

He would laugh each time and assure me he had written the song. He had this great smile, so big that it lit up his whole face. He threw his head back to laugh, too, and it was the most open and honest laugh I had heard in years. It occurred to me that I was falling in love. Or at least something very close.

When I glanced at my watch, I nearly had heart failure. I couldn't believe we'd been hiding away in Sharon's room for two whole hours! I was afraid she'd have a fit.

"I guess we should get back to the party," I suggested.

"It's probably just about over by now."

"Hey, what's your name, anyway?" I always hate asking people that. It sounds so contrived, somehow. I don't know why. Maybe because I'm used to meeting people in normal, everyday situations where their names just kind of become associated with them by circumstance. Like in school. You never ask anybody's name, but you always know who's who.

"Saul." He shook my hand, an act that I found totally charming.

"I'm Sallie Spooner. Do you go to our school? I don't remember having seen you."

"No. I live in Brooklyn. I'm just here in the city for the evening."

Coming from Boston, I always think it's funny when people who live in the other boroughs—Queens, the Bronx, Staten Island, or Brooklyn—refer to Manhattan as "the city." After all, to the rest of the world, *all* those places constitute New York City.

"How do you know Sharon, then?"

"I worked with her brother this summer. Construction."

"Oh." I looked at him more carefully. "Saul? What kind of name is that? I mean, I don't want to be rude or anything. . . ."

"It's okay." He smiled that smile again, hitting me with a view of two perfect rows of pearly whites. "It's really Saúl—it rhymes with Raúl." He pronounced it Sa-ool. "Only people outside my neighborhood call me 'Sol.' You know, like the sun."

"Oh." I guess I still looked confused. "What nationality is that? I never heard of . . ."

"It's Spanish. Or really Puerto Rican."

"You're Puerto Rican?" I don't know why, but I was flabbergasted.

"Yup. Saúl Rodriguez, when I'm in Brooklyn. In Manhattan, I'm just Saul, like Sol the sun god. It's easier that way."

"Did you always live in Brooklyn?" I asked cautiously.

"You mean, do I come from Puerto Rico?" he teased. He could tell I was having trouble digesting this whole situation. I turned red again. "No, I was born in Brooklyn. But my parents are both from Puerto Rico."

"Where do you live in Brooklyn?"

He tweaked my nose then and said, "It's not a very pretty

neighborhood. I bet a cute little girl from Manhattan like you never even heard of it.''

"Hey, wait a minute." Having my nose tweaked sets off the same reaction in me as being called Sal. I see red. "First of all, don't touch my nose. Second of all, I'm not from Manhattan; I'm from Boston, originally. And third, I don't appreciate you being so condescending.''

He looked surprised, maybe even hurt. "Hey, I'm sorry. I was just kidding. Still friends?'' He held out his hand again. I could feel the old familiar melting feeling starting up again.

"Friends." I shook his hand. "Wait a sec. Before we go back to the party, or whatever's left of it, can I ask you something?''

"Sure. What?''

"You know WROX, the rock music radio station?''

"Of course.''

"They're having a songwriting contest, and, well, I'm looking for somebody to collaborate with. Do you think maybe we could try writing a song together and enter the contest as a team?''

Saul thought about my offer for a few seconds, then said, "Sure. Why not?''

"Great!'' I told him where I lived, and he agreed to come over the very next day to see what we could come up with.

We went back to the living room. I was kind of disappointed that no one had even missed me. But I was also experiencing a bizarre kind of euphoria. I wasn't sure if it was the thrill of finally having found a musical partner, or having met someone as nice as Saul. One thing was for sure: the way my insides were jumping around and the way I started talking a mile a minute and laughing hysterically at every little thing made me wonder if perhaps there was such a thing as love at first sight after all.

4

The next day could not come soon enough. All night I dreamed about flashing white teeth and mysterious dark eyes. In the morning I washed my hair, even though it was still clean. I told myself that cleanliness is next to godliness. I kept having to remind myself that the reason Saul Rodriguez was coming over was to write music, not to live it.

"Mom," I said casually over our Saturday afternoon lunch of grilled-tuna-and-cheese sandwiches, "I have a friend coming over after lunch to work on songs. You know, for the WROX contest."

"That's nice, dear," she said dreamily. She seemed much more interested in scraping away at the melted cheese stain that Jenny's sandwich had predictably left on the tablecloth.

"That's great!" Jenny exclaimed. "So you finally found yourself a partner. See, I told you it would work out. Who is it?"

"Somebody I met at Sharon's last night."

"Male or female?"

I cast a dirty look at Jenny. Usually she's okay, but every

once in a while she starts acting like a little sister. Or maybe I was just being overly sensitive.

"It happens to be a person of the male persuasion," I answered coolly. "But let me assure you that my interest in him is purely professional."

"Hey, I never doubted it." Jenny sounded defensive, but I could see that she was hiding an impish grin behind her sandwich.

"What's his name, Sallie?" Mom had succeeded in getting rid of the cheese stain, so now she was ready to move on to more interesting concerns.

"His name is Saul."

My father looked up from his plate. "Saul? I've never heard of him before."

"Daddy, I just told you. I met him last night, at Sharon's party." I swear, sometimes I wonder how my parents manage to function in the outside world. It can take such a long time for things to register with them.

"Does he go to your school?" Mom asked. All of a sudden, I started getting irritated over the fact that Saul was becoming the main topic of conversation.

"No," I answered grumpily. "He's a friend of Sharon's brother."

"Oh, dear. How old is he, Sallie?"

"He's seventeen, just like me." Her concern was only natural, because Sharon's brother is an old man of twenty. I guess she was afraid I was going to start running around with some wild crowd. I could easily predict the questions that were to follow, so I went ahead and answered them in advance: "He's a senior in high school, lives in Brooklyn, is not and never has been a member of the Communist party."

"I think our Sallie is in love," Jenny said matter-of-factly as she reached across the table for the bowl of cole slaw.

"Jenny, hon, don't reach, *ask*," Mom interrupted. "And don't tease your sister."

"It doesn't bother me," I answered, keeping my cool. "She can say whatever she wants, because I know, in my heart of hearts, that Saul and I are just business associates."

"Saul," my father repeated. "What's his last name, Sallie?"

"What difference does that make?" I answered too quickly. My mother glanced up at me, surprised. Even Jenny remained silent.

"I just like to have some idea of who my daughter is hanging around with," Dad answered. "Not to mention who it is who comes to my home."

"I'm sorry. His name is Rodriguez. Saul Rodriguez." Suddenly self-conscious, I buried myself in my glass of milk. "He's Puerto Rican," I offered timidly.

"That's nice." Mom stood up and started clearing the table. "Jenny, since Sallie has company coming over, will you please help me with the lunch dishes, even though it's her turn? I'm sure she'll do your lunch dishes for you tomorrow."

"I'm going to see if I can fix that bathroom sink." My father sighed. "It's been dripping for days. The thing drives me crazy at night. It's all I can hear as I'm lying in bed, trying to sleep. Drip . . . drip . . . drip . . ."

It was odd to feel relieved. I was tempted to kick myself, but we all know that mental torture can be much effective than physical torture. I felt lousy over what had just transpired. Here, Saul was one of the sweetest, nicest people I had met in ages, and yet I had still felt that I had to apologize for his background.

"You don't deserve him as a friend," I told myself.

Still, by the time he showed up, all that had been forgotten. I was trying so hard not to be nervous that I had no time to ruminate over social issues. All I knew was that a guy I thought was pretty special would be showing up at my front door any minute, and I really wanted to impress him. I had even dragged out the lavender overalls again, because they have the power to make me feel beautiful and irresistible. Some women get that effect from expensive French perfume; for me, it's the feel of purple corduroy against my skin.

I must admit, though, that at that point, I was optimistic about our future together. Saul and Sallie. Sallie and Saul. There was certain poetry to the combination of our names that convinced me that we were destined to become more than just a crackerjack songwriting team. I have an overactive imagination, and by the time he appeared, I already had us married, a rich and famous musical duo that was the toast of two coasts.

"Hi, Sallie!" he said when I flung open the front door in response to his knock. "How's it going?" He was wearing his baggy jeans again, and a different plaid flannel shirt. His guitar was slung over his shoulder in a canvas case, as if he were some modern-day troubador.

"Terrific." No. I vowed right then and there never again to use that word in the presence of a male. "Fine. Come on in."

"Sallie, I think I heard someone at the front door. . . ." Jenny wandered in from the kitchen, where she and a couple of her friends were baking cookies for some school thing. She wore a look of complete innocence. "Oh, I'm sorry. I didn't realize you had company."

"Hello, Jenny." Saul beamed at my sister, then extended his hand. "I'm pleased to meet you."

Jenny shot me a triumphant look as she shook his hand. "So, you're a songwriter, too, huh? You know Sallie writes songs all the time."

I waited for her to say something cutting and little sisterish. Instead, she surprised me by coming out with, "My sister is a musical genius. And she tells me you're

pretty good, too. I'm expecting great things from you two."
I took that little speech to mean that she approved of Saul.

"We'll try not to disappoint you," Saul assured her.
"Any particular themes that are favorites of yours? We can
write according to specification, I'm sure."

"Hmm." Jenny frowned pensively. I could tell she was
really enjoying all this attention. I think that when you're a
younger sister, you must end up feeling slighted a lot of the
time, especially by your older sister's friends. "Love songs
are always nice." I wasn't sure, but I thought I saw her
wink at me.

"Okay, we'll try. But first let me ask you one thing."
"What?"

Saul leaned over until he was at eye level with Jenny.
"Why is it your sister has red hair, and yours is blond?" He
tugged gently on one of the pigtails she had braided her hair
into after lunch.

"Because blonds have more fun," Jenny answered
smugly. She grinned at Saul, then turned on her heel and
disappeared back into the kitchen.

"I think you just made my sister fall in love with you,
you heartbreaker," I teased as I led him down the hall. "Is it
okay if we work in my room? It's probably the quietest spot
in the house."

"Fine with me."

We settled into my room, sitting cross-legged on the
floor.

"Well," I began, "you've already heard just about every
song I've ever written, so you know all about the kind of
stuff I write."

"The same goes for me. I think we should start by
deciding what kind of song we'll write. You know: fast or
slow, romantic or something else, optimistic or sad."

I thought for a minute. "Maybe we should take Jenny's
advice and go with a love song."

I was kind of disappointed that Saul was so eager to get down to business. If all we ever did was talk about music, I'd never get to know him better. It was true that my main purpose in getting together with him was to advance my musical career, but I figured that a little socializing never hurt.

"That's a good place to start," he agreed. "Let's see, a love song. Hmm. I don't know about you, but I'm tired of really depressing songs about love affairs that have failed. You know, all those sad lyrics about being lonely and sitting by the phone and broken hearts. I'd like to try for something more upbeat, something hopeful."

"Yeah, I know what you mean. Although those songs about how great somebody else is can get to sound the same, too. How about a theme of a love affair that's just getting started, so everybody's hopeful, but there are enough complications that the couple has to overcome some obstacles?"

"That sounds perfect. Then we could make it kind of fast. Not heavy rock, but something that moves along." Saul picked up his guitar and took it out of its canvas case. "Something like this, maybe." He plucked out a few chords, using a beat that was zippy, but not *too* zippy.

"I love it. That's the mood we should look for." I could feel myself growing excited. "And it should have some catchy harmony, too."

"Sallie, when we enter this contest, who's going to perform the song? I mean, that's how you enter, right? There's a live, onstage competition and not just tapes?"

"That's right. Why? Do you get stage fright?" I joked.

"Not at all. In fact, I'm a real ham when it comes to playing in front of an audience. Just give me one listener, voluntary or otherwise, and there's no stopping me."

"Well, then, maybe we should decide right now who's going to perform the song at the competition."

"I think we both should, don't you? Especially if we're going to build in all that catchy harmony you were just talking about."

"Good," I said, relieved. "I was afraid we might end up disagreeing on that."

Saul grew very serious. "Hey, look, Sallie, we're an equal partnership, right? We split everything fifty-fifty, including both the work and the rewards. That's the deal as I understood it, and that's how I intend to do this whole thing."

He returned to his fooling around on the guitar.

"Saul," I began, pulling my guitar out from under the bed, its official residence, so that I, too, could plunk around, trying to fall upon a melody, "how did you get started writing songs?"

He shrugged, and without even stopping his distracted picking at the strings, said, "I don't really know. I've been into music for as long as I can remember. A lot of the guys in my neighborhood are." He paused as he concentrated on a particular chord progression, his head bobbing in time to the beat. "Maybe I always kind of considered it a way out, too."

"A way out of what?"

"The whole thing of living in Brooklyn in a neighborhood that is about as far away from this neighborhood"—he glanced around my room—"as you can get. This guy, Juan, who's my best friend, has an older brother who just went on tour as a backup musician for Yes. And then this other guy I know, Luis, has a job as a studio musician. He's a drummer." He stopped talking for a minute, then started playing "Here Comes the Sun" again.

"At least he *was* a drummer. He got cut up pretty bad in a fight last weekend. His hand is all bandaged up now. I don't know how long it'll be before he can go back to work again."

"What happened?" I tried not to look too shocked. Fortunately Saul's eyes were on his fingers as they darted from fret to fret, from string to string, and not on old Sallie Spooner's round, staring eyes.

"Nothing, really. He was just hanging out with some of his friends last Saturday night, drinking beer and smoking a couple of joints, around the corner from where I live. Some guys came by, and the next thing you know, Luis ends up with a sliver of glass from a broken bottle in the palm of his right hand."

"But who *were* they?" I couldn't get over how matter-of-fact Saul sounded about the whole thing.

"I don't know. Just some guys."

"Guys they knew, you mean, or strangers?"

At that point he turned his full attention toward me. "Sallie, surely you've been on the subways. Surely you've read the papers. I expect that you know there is more to the world than the Upper East Side of Manhattan, with its poodles and limousines and ladies in fur coats." He didn't sound nasty at all; he just sounded surprised that I was asking so many questions and acting so appalled.

"It must be a rough neighborhood," was all I could think of to say.

"Yeah, but I don't expect to stay there forever. Which brings us back to your original question of how I got started writing songs."

"But surely there's more to it than that! It's not just a way to get you away from Brooklyn, is it?"

"No, of course not. I love music, and I happen to be lucky enough to be pretty good at it. I can hardly think of a time when there wasn't a radio playing somewhere in the background. Music's been a part of my life for as long as I can remember. All kinds, too: rock, jazz, salsa . . ."

I started getting restless. "Saul, are you always so serious?" I asked in a teasing voice.

"About music, I am," he answered earnestly. "But there are other times . . ." He grabbed my foot and pulled it up into the air, then started making noises like a monkey. I immediately convulsed with giggles.

"Stop! Stop!" I screeched between my hyena-like screams. "I was only kidding!"

With a fake Spanish accent, Saul cried, "I weel show you no mercy until you agree to marry my seester!"

When I couldn't breathe anymore and I was just about ready to faint from laughing so hard, he finally let go of my foot.

"You're a nut!" I told him, still laughing.

"That's nothing. You haven't seen my Al Pacino imitation yet."

"Saul, tell me something. I probably sound ridiculously sheltered and naive, but you've got to understand . . ."

"That you *are* sheltered and naive. What do you want to ask me?"

I lowered my voice and narrowed my eyes into tiny slits. "Do you carry a knife to school?"

"Why, do you think all Puerto Ricans have knives in their pointed black shoes?"

"I didn't mean . . ." My voice faltered.

"Hey, look, I was only kidding," Saul said quickly. "You know, I don't mind making jokes about being Puerto Rican. There is such a thing as taking yourself too seriously, you know. I think everybody should be able to fool around about themselves and their background. I mean, I could very easily make jokes about your orange hair, right?"

I gripped a strand of hair self-consciously and wrapped it around my finger.

"Just as long as it's all meant in fun, and not maliciously," he went on. "I know what people think about Puerto Ricans in this day and age. Especially people who live in New York. There are stereotypes about them, just as there are about every other ethnic group, not to mention any other kind of group you can think of. All I have to do is say 'Save the whale,' and immediately a certain type of person comes to mind, right? Well, it's the same thing. Everybody has preconceived notions about everything, especially other people. Some are based on fact, and some on fantasy. What's important is keeping an open mind."

"I can tell you've given this a lot of thought," I ventured, still unsure of how to react.

"Yup, the old boy is thinking all the time. But seriously, Sallie, you can ask me anything want to know."

"Okay."

"And I would hope that I could feel free to do the same."

"It's only fair."

Saul leaned forward and said, in a soft, conspiratorial voice, "So, tell me, where's the bathroom in this joint?"

After that, the ice between Saul and me was completely broken. It was amazing how comfortable I felt with him, and how quickly. Besides, we had so much in common. Despite our noble intentions, we ended up talking away the rest of the afternoon. We talked about different rock groups; we talked about writing songs; we listened to a few of my new record albums. The chemistry was definitely there.

The only negative was that we never did get started on a song. I guess the inspiration simply wasn't there. We agreed to stick to our original plan of an upbeat love song, but neither of us seemed to have any ideas.

"It'll come," Saul assured me.

When there was a knock at the door, I called "Come in!" I turned to look over in that direction, and as I did, I got a glimpse of the clock on my dresser. Five o'clock! I couldn't believe it was so late; the afternoon had flown right by. Again. A weird trend seemed to be emerging: Whenever I was with Saul, I lost all track of time. Did this mean something?

It was Jenny who was standing in the doorway. "Hi, Sallie. Hi, Saul. How's it going?"

Saul and I glanced at each other.

"We're getting there," he assured her, winking at me.

"Do I get a preview?"

"Not yet," I said. "Not until it's perfect."

"Well, just as long as I'm the very first person who gets to hear your creation. Mom wants to know if Saul's staying for dinner."

I looked over at him, but he was shaking his head and putting his guitar back into its case.

"Thanks a lot, but I'm afraid I can't. I have to get going."

"Maybe some other time?" I said hastily.

"Yeah, that'd be great."

"Okay. I'll tell Mom." Jenny ran off.

As Saul got his stuff together to leave, I started feeling all shy and weak-kneed again. "So when can we get together again? I mean, to work on this song."

"I guess we didn't get very far today, did we?" Saul grinned at me, and I knew I was going to have another night full of dreams about that beautiful, honest face. "When do you want to get together?"

Anytime. I was tempted to say, "Take me—I'm yours." But instead, I cleared my throat and said, "How about Tuesday night?"

"That sounds fine. Only next time, *we work*!"

"Okay," I agreed, smiling. "Why don't you come over around seven-thirty?"

"Right. See you then. And if you come up with anything inspired, be sure to write it down. We've still got a lot to get done on this prize-winning song that's going to guarantee us both a Grammy Award!"

On the way out Saul had to pass through the living room, where my parents had discreetly placed themselves. He met them both, and I got the impression that they approved. Jenny, too, continued hanging around him as if he were some movie star or something.

When he had gone, I started back to my bedroom. I could hear Jenny saying to my parents, in a voice that was intentionally loud enough for me to hear, "Well, I don't know if Sallie is falling in love with Saul Rodriguez, but I can assure you that *I* am!"

I was glad I was safely inside my bedroom by then, so that no one could see me blush.

5

Because Rachel and I are best friends—as well as soul mates, blood sisters, and spiritual twins—I usually tell her everything I do, think, say, and feel. Even though we see each other at least once a day in school, we generally end up spending an hour or so on the phone together every night. Sometimes it seems that the best part about having something exciting happen to me is telling Rachel about it later on. When I found out that I was going to win the Most Musical Award at the end of my sophomore year, when Mike Ferguson, an old crush from a million years ago, asked me to the junior prom, when I finally got permission from my mom to get my ears pierced, my thoughts were always the same: "I can't wait to tell Rachel!"

For some reason this was not the case with one Saul Rodriguez. It's not that I was hiding anything from her; it's just that there was something so sacred, so *fragile*, about having discovered Saul so unexpectedly in the middle of Sharon Burke's duller-than-dull party that I was afraid to talk about it. Even to Rachel. It was like betraying a confidence, in some strange way.

Ordinarily I would have felt guilty about holding out on

Rachel, especially about something as important as budding love. But as it turned out, the next few days were pretty busy ones for both of us, and the only conversations we had were hasty and superficial.

"How was Sharon's party?" she called to me on Monday morning as I was running to music theory and she was trekking over to the language lab.

"It was okay."

"Good. I'll call you later."

But she never did, because of some last-minute quiz that was scheduled for Tuesday. I was relieved, in a way, that things were ending up that way. I preferred to be left on my own, to daydream, to plan, and to moon over this new stranger who had wandered into my life from Brooklyn, of all places.

So lost was I in my own little world, in fact, that I was actually surprised to hear Rachel's voice when I answered the telephone that Tuesday night at exactly seven-twenty-two.

"Hi, Sallie? It's me, Rachel. How are you? I feel like I haven't talked to you in ages!"

"I know. I guess I've been busy the last couple of days."

"Me, too. And now I'm drowning in *Don Quixote*. Spanish test tomorrow. *Already!* It's only the third week of classes, and already I'm swamped."

"They don't waste any time, that's for sure." I glanced at my watch nervously. Seven-twenty-four.

"I wanted to ask you a favor, though. You know my English notebook, the one I lent you last week? I need it back right away. I found out today that I have to give a little talk on *Moby Dick* tomorrow in class, and all my notes are in it. Do you think maybe you could drop it off tonight? It's kind of an emergency. . . ."

"Uh . . ." Seven-twenty-five. At any minute Saul would be at my front door, guitar in hand. But then it occurred to me that it might be kind of fun to surprise

Rachel. "Sure, I'll bring it over. But is it okay if someone else comes with me?"

"Who? Jenny?"

"No. It's a surprise. Someone you've never met before."

"It's fine with me. I just washed my hair, but if this mystery person doesn't mind getting dripped on, I certainly don't care."

"Okay. We'll be by in around fifteen minutes."

I hung up, wondering what Rachel's reaction to Saul would be. I hoped they would like each other. There is nothing worse than having the people you care most about going at each other like cats and dogs.

Once again I had an ugly thought: Perhaps it would bother Rachel that Saul was Puerto Rican. There was no reason why it should, as far as I knew. But still, I was suddenly keenly aware of the current status of New York's social scene. Well, the solution to that was simple enough. I just wouldn't tell her. I'd let her get to know him first, let her see what a terrific guy he was. There was nothing wrong with that. I mean, I don't exactly go around introducing my friends to each other by saying, "This is Rachel. She's Jewish." Or "This is Dan, he's German."

Promptly at seven-thirty the doorbell rang, and there was Saul. Once again, I had dressed in that special style that I call "conscientious-casual." I knew that the excitement of seeing him again was bringing a sparkle to my eyes and a flush to my cheeks. I had noticed that about myself lately; every time I looked into a mirror, I appeared to be glowing. It was most becoming, I thought.

"Hi, Sallie! All set for a night of hard work?"

"You bet. But first I have to do a quick errand. Do you mind if we run over to a friend's house for a minute? I have to drop something off. It's only a few blocks away, and we won't have to stay very long."

"It's fine with me."

He deposited his guitar in my room, and after scrounging

around my desk for a few minutes, I came up with Rachel's notebook.

"All set?" he asked, and we set off for the Glasses' apartment.

"The person you're about to meet is my best friend in the whole world. Her name is Rachel Glass. People are always kidding us about our last names. Glass and Spooner. Get it? Anyway, she's been my best friend ever since I moved to New York, just about."

I proceeded to fill Saul in on my entire history as we walked over to Rachel's. It was a lovely evening, I remember, with that balmy feeling of late Indian summer. But the promise of autumn was unmistakable. That's my favorite time of the year, I think. Early fall. And then early spring is nice, too. I think when the seasons are just about to change from very hot to very cold, and vice versa, it makes the air seem fresher and the world seem brand-new. It was exhilarating, and I was out of breath by the time we reached East Seventy-seventh Street.

"This is it," I announced, leading Saul past the doorman, who considers me an honorary resident of his building. We rode the elevator up to the twentieth floor.

As we stood outside the front door of the Glasses' apartment waiting for it to be opened, I had a quick fit of nervousness. What if Saul and Rachel hated each other on sight? I thought once again. It was possible, after all. And it would make my life difficult, as I tried to juggle two adversaries who were both near and dear to me.

It was Rachel who answered the door. True to her word, her hair was sopping wet, and it hung about her head like a veil. You know the way Victor Mature looks in those old French Foreign Legion movies they always show on TV on Sunday afternoons? The ones where he looks like he's wearing a dish towel on his head? That was what immediately came to mind as I saw her standing there. Her wet wavy locks were causing little dark spots to form on the collar of her pink T-shirt. She was wearing her scrungiest jeans and had no shoes on. The look in her eyes was one of distraction, and I could tell that she had been lost in the magical world of *Don Quixote*. In Spanish, no less.

But a curious thing happened. The instant she laid eyes on Saul, her expression changed. It softened—or rather, it *melted*—right before my eyes. I wasn't sure what was happening, so I glanced over at him. He, too, had suddenly developed that dreamy look. The two of them just stared at each other for what seemed an eternity, with neither of them saying anything. The whole thing was a bit embarrassing, if you ask me.

"Hi, Rachel," I said, feeling obligated to break the unusual silence that seemed to have gripped everyone all of a sudden. "Uh, I'd like you to meet Saul, a friend of mine. Saul, this is Rachel."

Their eyes never left each other. "Hello, Rachel," Saul said. In his usual fashion, he shook her hand. But somehow, the crisp friendliness that generally accompanied that action was nowhere to be found. Instead, they sort of clung to each other. I thought maybe I was imagining the whole thing, however, so I went on in my brusque, cheerful manner.

"Saul and I are working on a song together. We're going to enter it in the WROX contest. I told you all about that, Rachel, didn't I? He and I met at Sharon's party Saturday night, and we decided to try working together. Anyway, here's your notebook. Sorry about keeping it for such a long time."

We engaged in a few more minutes of small talk, still standing there in the hallway. Fortunately, Saul and Rachel both chimed in eventually. It was nothing significant, just your usual cocktail party conversation. Finally, I insisted that Saul and I had to return to our songwriting. It was getting late, and quite frankly, I was getting a bit worried about the low level of productivity of our songwriting team. After all, time was getting short.

As Saul and I walked back to my place, he seemed sort of quiet. I already knew him well enough to realize that that was an unusual state for him. But I filled in the silences by chattering away about Rachel and my long friendship with her. Saul was proving to be a good listener.

"Well, shall we settle down and get some work done?" I asked when we were back at home. "I'm afraid I haven't come up with anything since Saturday. I've been kind of busy with other things. How about you?"

We were back on the floor of my room, our guitars standing by, ready and waiting. Once I mentioned our still-unwritten song, in my serious, no-nonsense tone of voice, Saul snapped back to the present from whichever planet he had been on temporarily.

"Oh, didn't I tell you?" he said, picking up his guitar and turning his attention back to music. "I came up with the beginnings of a melody that we might use."

He picked out a few bars of a really catchy tune. There was a nice chord accompaniment to go with it, too. It was just what I had imagined, exactly what I had hoped for.

"That's it!" I cried. "Saul, you're a true genius!"

"But that's just the beginning," he insisted. "We need much more than that."

"Hmm. How about something like this?" I picked up my guitar and played what he had just shown me, then added on a bit more.

"Perfect! And then, it could go into something like this. . . ."

The melody just flowed out of our two guitars. We sounded like Dueling Banjos as we echoed each other, back and forth, each time adding on another measure, coming up with a different chord or some inspired harmony. Within an hour, we had come up with a first-rate song.

"That was so simple!" I exclaimed once we were satisfied with the music. "You were right. It *did* come. And so easily, too. It's as if the song was floating around in this room, and all we had to do was find it and tie it down. Like helium balloons."

"You're kind of poetic, aren't you?" Saul teased. "And it's a good thing. You may not have noticed, but our wonderful little song has no lyrics yet."

"Oh, yeah. I forgot about that. Lyrics." I studied the floor. Whereas the musical inspiration had blossomed, wild and free, the words just would not come. "It should be easier to think of words, now that we've got the melody. You know how these things just follow naturally."

"I hope so," Saul sighed. "At the moment, I can't think of a single thing."

There was a timid knock at the door, one that I recognized immediately as Jenny's. She poked her head in at my invitation.

"I don't want to disturb you guys," she apologized, "but as I was coming out of the bathroom, I heard wonderful sounds coming from this room. Is it possible that a song—or rather, *the* song—has been born?"

"Well, half of it," I said.

"Which half?"

"The music half. The words have not yet found their way into our creative little brains."

Jenny's eyes opened wide. "Oooh, do you think I can hear what you've written? I promise to like it!" She came into my room cautiously, as if she really was afraid she was bothering us. I had to admit that she looked cute in her yellow terrycloth bathrobe and embroidered Deerfoam slippers, with her cheeks all pink and dewy from her bath. Her hair was in braids again. It seemed that ever since Saul had tweaked them on Saturday afternoon, she had been wearing braids every minute of the day.

"What do you say, partner?" Saul asked me. "I already told you how I feel about audiences. It doesn't take much to get me started."

"If you think we're ready for our debut."

We launched into an energetic rendition of our new song, singing and harmonizing with the words, "Da da da." When we were done, we looked to Jenny for her reaction.

"It's fantastic!" she squealed. "I love it! When can I buy the record?"

"Now, wait a minute," Saul said seriously. "You said before that you promised to like this song, no matter what. We want your *honest* reaction."

"I swear! I love it!" Jenny insisted.

"Will you stick to that opinion, even under the tickle torture?" he asked, still using that serious tone.

"Oh, no, not that!" she squealed, looking a bit nervous.

Saul glanced at me, a mischievous look in his eye. I returned his grin, then the two of us descended upon Jenny, tickling her mercilessly.

"I love it! I love it!" she yelped, over and over again.

"You love being tickled?" I cried.

"No, no! I love the song! I *hate* being tickled!"

When we, her two tormenters, were convinced that she meant what she said, we finally relented.

"I guess she means it," Saul said matter-of-factly as Jenny tried to regain her composure and start breathing normally again. "She even withstood the tickle torture."

"Well, Mr. Rodriguez," I said, "I'd say we have a hit on our hands!"

"If they love it in New York," Jenny said, "they'll love it everywhere. And to show you how much I like it, I'll even give you guys some of the cookies I made on Saturday."

"Are these leftovers?" I asked as she dragged us both to the kitchen.

"Not at all," she assured us. "These are the special ones, the ones with the extra chocolate chips that I put aside. Just in case you guys came up with a hit. See, I believe that creativity deserves material rewards, as well as spiritual ones."

Saul went home a while later, after we both promised each other that we would make lyrics the most important thing in our lives until we finished the song. One thing we were both sure of: we would have to come up with some pretty terrific words to go with the wonderful melody we had written.

After he'd left, I happily retired to the bathroom to wash my face and brush my teeth. I was feeling really good, about our song, about Saul, about life in general. I even noticed that, thanks to Dr. Glass and his magic dermatological powers, my skin was looking as creamy as an English baroness's.

I was just about to climb into bed when the telephone rang. It was so late that I figured the call was for one of my parents, so I didn't bother charging out into the hall the way I usually did. Instead, I got under the covers, ready to succumb to my growing tiredness and mull over the events of the day.

So I was surprised when my mother came to my door and said, "Sallie? Are you still awake? Telephone. It's Rachel."

I threw on my old turquoise chenille bathrobe and went out into the hall.

"Rachel? What's up?"

"Were you asleep, Sallie? I'm sorry."

"No, no. I had just gotten into bed."

"Because I could talk to you tomorrow in school. . . ."

"No, no," I assured her again. "It's okay. Why? What's up?"

"Sallie, the weirdest thing just happened."

"Really? What?" I settled into the chair that's next to the telephone table, prepared for some really hot gossip.

"Saul just called me and asked me out for Friday night."

"*What*?" I couldn't believe I was hearing her correctly.

Surely there was some mistake! Perhaps I was sleepier than I had realized.

"You know, Saul. The guy you introduced me to tonight. He just called from a pay phone. He was on the way to the subway, he said, and he wanted to call me before it got too late."

"How did he get your number?" Although all my tiredness had vanished, I was feeling dazed.

"In the telephone book. I mean, he knew my last name, and he knew that I live on East Seventy-seventh Street. Look, I'm as surprised about this as you are."

"Well, what did you say?"

"Oh, nothing much. It was a short conversation."

"No, I mean about going out with him Friday night." I was gripping the receiver so tightly that it was slipping out of my sweaty palm.

"I said yes, of course. I don't really know the guy, but I kind of like the idea of going out with him." She paused, then added a bit dreamily, "We're going to the movies."

I cleared my throat. "Well, that's great, Rach. I'm very happy for you. Saul is a terrific guy."

There was a dead silence. Then Rachel said, "Oh, Sallie, *you're* not interested in him, are you? I assumed that you guys were just working on songs together, but if you had something else in mind . . ."

"Oh, no," I assured her. "My interest in Saul is purely professional." I sounded so convincing that I almost believed myself. But the fact that my heart was beating a trillion times a minute was a dead giveaway. "I mean, he's a nice guy, and he is kind of cute. . . ."

"Because if you want to go out with him, I certainly won't."

"No, go out with him. He obviously likes you a lot. He even tracked down your phone number." The hallway had become a total blur.

"Gee, I'm glad you feel that way," Rachel said,

sounding all dreamy again. "Because I'm really excited about going out with him. Sallie, how well do you know him?"

"Not very well at all. Why?"

"Because I have this funny feeling that Saul is . . . I don't know, *different* from the other guys we know who are our age. Remember our double date with Dan and Fred?"

"How could I ever forget?" I groaned. "That experience has warped me for life."

"Well, you know what I mean, then. Those guys are so immature, so irresponsible . . . and I have this uncanny feeling that Saul isn't like that at all. He seems so . . . so *stable*."

"Maybe. I don't know him that well."

Rachel sighed. "I don't know how I'll ever manage to fall asleep tonight. See, my mom was right. It's just a question of time before we meet nice, *mature* boys. Oh, Sallie, I hope you start going out with somebody like Saul, too!"

"Yeah," I said glumly. "Well, look, I'd better hit the sack. Big French test tomorrow."

"Okay. See you in school! And Sallie?"

"Yeah?"

"Thanks for introducing me to Saul. I know you weren't trying to match us up or anything . . . but thanks just the same. I have this feeling that things are going to work out really well for us."

"Sure. Anytime. Bye, Rachel. See you tomorrow."

That night it took me a long time to fall asleep. Maybe it was because I was confused, maybe it was because I was stunned—or maybe it was because I knew I wouldn't be dreaming about mischievous grins and dark mustaches anymore.

6

Whenever I get upset or depressed or otherwise disturbed, there are two things I do. The first is to take long walks around New York City. There is no better way to forget your own troubles than by traipsing around the Lower East Side, for example, where Mott Street, the heart of Chinatown, runs parallel to Mulberry Street, whose cappuccino bars and bakeries transport you to Italy. Or Spring Street, filled with galleries and poster shops and tiny bookstores that look as if they got stuck in a time warp and still think it's 1968. Even my own neighborhood is fun to poke around in. It seems as if every time I stroll down Second Avenue, there's some new store or restaurant that didn't exist until five minutes earlier, when it magically sprang up out of nowhere.

The whole week after I discovered that Saul had asked Rachel out, I did a lot of walking. I also did a lot of eating, my second way of dealing with bad moods. The rest of Jenny's cookies were the very first to go. After that I became less selective. Anything would do. Besides eating and walking, I found myself avoiding Rachel. I pretended I had a big test to study for, when in reality the only test I had was the test to see how many Oreos one person could consume at one sitting.

It was Jenny, the cookie monger herself, who eventually came to my rescue. On Friday evening, the night that I knew Saul and Rachel would be painting the town red while I was left behind, she found me putting my jacket on around seven in the evening, the dating hour.

"Where are you going?" she asked congenially.

"I thought I'd hike over to Ray's and get myself a couple of slices of pizza. That way I can indulge in both my favorite pastimes, eating and walking, in one fell swoop."

"I'll come with you," she offered, ducking into her room to retrieve a heavy sweater.

"I thought you were going to paint tonight," I said, a trifle crossly. I have never relished the idea of being pitied, especially by a thirteen-year-old.

"It can wait. I've lost my inspiration. Besides, a piece of pizza sounds like a good idea. I love Mom dearly, but her meat loaf is not exactly known as one of New York's finer delicacies."

The two of us started across town, over to Ray's.

"It's a nice evening," Jenny noted cheerfully.

"I wish it would rain." I'm afraid that I was scowling.

"Perhaps you'd like to tell me about it." Sometimes Jenny amazes me, she's so serene and well adjusted. Suddenly I realized that while her ears were not particularly experienced, they would be sympathetic and possibly even consoling.

"It's Saul."

"Oh. I thought it might be." She paused as we moved aside to make room on the sidewalk for a wheezing jogger. "I'd noticed he hasn't been around lately."

"We're still writing our song for the contest. It's just

that . . . well, he asked Rachel out. Tonight's their first date."

"Rachel? *Our* Rachel? Rachel Glass?"

I nodded. "None other."

"But she's your best friend! Is nothing sacred anymore?"

"Relax, Jen. She had no idea I was interested in him." I sighed deeply. I had to admit, it felt good telling someone what had been on my mind all week. It certainly beat being stoic and holding it in. Or trying to eat it away. "Look, the way I feel—at least rationally—is that Saul met both of us, and he picked Rachel. It's not her fault, and it's not his fault. It's just . . . life."

"Hmm. It sounds like a tough situation. I'll tell you one thing, though, Sallie. I like Saul a lot. But I'd hate to see your friendship with Rachel jeopardized, over *anything*. I mean, you two are practically twins, for heaven's sake."

"I know. That's what I keep reminding myself. And in a way, maybe it was inevitable. Rachel and I are so much alike that it stands to reason that we'd both be attracted to the same type of guy. But you're right. My friendship with Rachel can withstand anything, even this. It's too important to me, and that's all there is to it."

"That's the spirit! There'll be a lot of men in your life, but best friends are hard to come by. What's that Dorothy Parker said? 'Men are like streetcars; if you miss one, there'll be another one coming along soon.'"

We both laughed, and I started to feel better. Jenny was right, of course; I had never doubted it. Not for a second had I had any intention of letting Saul—or any other guy— come between Rachel and me. It would just take a while to get used to this whole thing. I knew I'd learn to live with it. Besides, I still had Saul as a friend and musical partner.

I was still marveling over how rational and well adjusted I was being the next day when I took advantage of a brisk Saturday morning to stroll through Carl Schurz Park, along the East River. Actually, I'm fooling myself if I pretend that I was merely seeking fresh air. After all, I was *walking*, one of my two great escapes, and it was around the time I expected that Rachel would call me with all the juicy details of her night on the town with Saul. Well, I never said I was *perfect*.

So there I was, hanging out with the joggers and the loiterers and the other casual strollers. I was taking in the view, which is not particularly pleasant, since it happens to be the small factories of Queens. As I stared into the murky waters of the East River, I heard a familiar voice calling my name: "Sallie! Sallie!" Actually it was more like a semihysterical shriek. I turned around and saw Rachel running toward me. I couldn't tell by her contorted face if it was very good news or very bad news that had brought her out to Carl Schurz Park on this fine September morning.

"Well, hi, Rachel," I said calmly, my arms spread out across the iron railing as if the park were my own living room. "How'd you know I was here?"

"I was just over at your apartment. Your mother told me where to find you." She was all out of breath.

"You're certainly up and out early this morning."

"Sallie, I have to talk to you."

It was at that point that it became clear to me that the news that had prompted Rachel's dramatic histrionics was bad news. I braced myself.

"Yeah? What's up?"

There was fire in her eyes as she stood before me, her hands on her hips, her mouth twisted into an angry frown.

"Sallie, Saul is Puerto Rican!"

Was *that* all? By that point I was so used to that fact that it was beyond my comprehension that anyone could possibly be fazed by it.

"Yes, I know." I wasn't trying to be irritating; I just couldn't help sounding matter-of-fact.

"You know? You *know*? Then why didn't you *tell* me?"

"Why didn't I tell you? Why should I have told you? There are a lot of things people know about each other that they don't bother to go around telling the whole world."

"Come on, Sallie. You know what I mean." She insisted upon maintaining that same pose. I was starting to feel uncomfortable. It was becoming clearer and clearer to me that Rachel really was serious about all this.

"All right, I suppose I could have told you. But to tell you the truth, I never even thought of it."

"Well, maybe you should have!"

"First of all, calm down, Rachel. People are looking at us. Second of all, what's the big deal?"

"Why, Saul and I are from entirely different backgrounds. . . ."

"You mean he's not Jewish."

"Well, yes. . . ."

"Plus there's the fact that being Puerto Rican is not exactly the most stylish thing to be these days."

"Sallie, you know I'm not a snob. It's just that . . . To tell you the truth, it's my parents I'm worried about. My mother and father would freak out if they knew I was going out with someone who's not only not Jewish, but who's Puerto Rican!"

"I can't believe you're saying this! What about the fact that Saul happens to be a fantastic guy? And you and I both know how hard those are to come by."

Rachel shook her head slowly. "You should have warned me."

I turned away and stared back at Queens and the river. The view was actually starting to look good to me, which I took as a bad sign.

"Well, then, Rachel, I guess at this point, you have two alternatives. You can either ignore the fact that Saul is Puerto Rican and remember the night you *thanked* me for introducing him to you, or you can refuse to see him anymore, and we can forget that the whole thing ever happened."

There were tears in her eyes as she looked over at me and said, "I'm afraid I can't see him again, Sallie."

"Is that really what you want?" I could hardly believe what I was hearing.

"What I really want has nothing to do with it. It's my parents. Not only them, but also everything they've ever taught me. It's centuries of history, it's a whole tradition . . . Oh, you wouldn't understand."

"I guess maybe I wouldn't." I glanced at her coldly. "Rachel, what exactly happened last night, anyway?"

She started to look uncomfortable at that point, and she shuffled around awkwardly. "Let me see. We started out by having a nice time. He came over and then we went to a movie, right here on Eighty-sixth Street. It wasn't until afterward that we started talking about . . . you know, our backgrounds."

"Go on."

"For heaven's sake, Sallie. His name is *Saul.* Saul is generally a Jewish name, so I just assumed he was Jewish.

"Anyway, we went out for something to eat. We were sitting in the coffee shop on the corner of First Avenue, and all of a sudden I realized that I didn't even know the guy's last name. So I asked him."

"And?"

"And he told me."

"And?"

"Well, I didn't insult him or anything! What do you think I am? Do you think I would just get up and run out or something childish like that?"

"At this point I have no idea." I looked at her with as piercing a look as I could manage.

"Thanks a lot." If looks could kill, I'd be floating around the East River right now, probably bobbing along somewhere near the Fifty-ninth Street Bridge. "We left soon afterward. He walked me home, and that was it."

"Did he kiss you good-night?"

"No, I ran inside before that could come up."

"Did he say he'd call you again?"

"Yes." She studied the back of her hand as if it had the key to the mysteries of life engraved on it. "I figured that if and when he calls me, I'll explain."

"Explain what? That he's not good enough for you?" My voice was positively dripping with sarcasm.

"Oh, Sallie! Can't you at least *try* to see things from my point of view?"

But I was beyond trying to be understanding. "I'll tell you something, Rachel Glass!" I practically screamed at her. "Right now, I think that *you're* not good enough for *him*!"

"Sallie," she returned in an equally loud and enthusiastic voice, "you have no idea what being Jewish is all about!"

"If it means cutting yourself off from other people—especially nice, good people like Saul—I'm completely turned off to it."

"Well, I don't think you're being very reasonable or very understanding. And I'll tell *you* something: I hold you fully responsible for getting me into this."

"Into *what*?"

"I already told you. You should have warned me. You owed me that much."

"Wait a minute," I said slowly, my eyes narrowing into slits. It was as if, all of a sudden, I had had a vision. The truth of what was actually going on hit me like the proverbial ton of bricks.

"The reason you're so upset about all this is that you really *like* Saul, don't you?"

"You don't have to sound so accusing," Rachel pouted.

"Oh, *I* see. If he had turned out to be some jerk, like Dan or Fred, we wouldn't even be having this discussion. But you're in real conflict over this one, aren't you?"

Rachel looked at me, her eyes flashing. "As I said before, Sallie Spooner, if you had had the sense to warn me of what was going on here, all this never would have happened. And if that's all you think of our friendship, then we might as well throw it into the East River, along with all the other garbage!"

She stormed off, her entire body tense with anger. I watched her stalk away, and I could feel myself growing mildly nauseated. Ten minutes before, I had been feeling bad because I had just lost a terrific guy. And now, on top of that, I had just lost my best friend.

Both walking and eating seemed useless at that point. I left the park, dragging my feet as though my sneakers had been cast in bronze. I felt as if I wanted only to be alone—possibly for the rest of my entire life—but when I reached my block and saw Jenny in front of our apartment building putting on her roller skates, I was overjoyed. At last, a friendly face!

"Hi, Jen. Got a minute?" I sauntered over to the curb, where she was spinning her wheels to see if they needed oiling.

"For you, kid, anytime. By the way, Rachel was here a while ago, looking for you. Mom told her you were at the park. Did you two ever meet up with each other?" She glanced up at me, then gasped, "What happened to you? You look terrible!"

"Do I look as if I just lost my best friend? Because I did."

"Oh, Sallie, what happened?" she repeated.

I proceeded to relate our whole dialogue to her, word for word. When I was through, she shook her head sympathetically and said, "Gee, that's really tough, Sallie. But you've got to keep this in perspective. You haven't done anything wrong. You're not to blame for anything."

"I know."

"And Rachel's the one who's acting ridiculous. If she wants to act all screwy over this thing with Saul, it has nothing to do with you."

"But she's my best friend! Or, she *was*. Now, she hates me."

"Oh, she doesn't hate you. You wait and see. She'll come around. She'll end up missing you as much as you miss her. Separating you guys would be like tearing Siamese twins apart." I gave Jenny my hand and helped her stand up on the sidewalk.

"I don't know. She's really upset about this."

"*Trust* me, Sallie. I know you, and I know Rachel. This will pass. In no time at all, you two will be spending hours on the phone giggling every night, just like old times."

"I hope you're right," I said doubtfully. I wanted to believe Jenny, but at that point the future was looking very bleak.

"Look, I've got to run. Or rather, I've got to roll. I'm meeting a couple of my friends over in front of the school. We're taking a skating tour of the neighborhood."

Unlike her older sister, Jenny Spooner is a terrific skater. She gave me a quick peck on the cheek, then glided away. I stood there on the sidewalk in front of my building, watching her until she turned the corner and disappeared. It was silly, I knew, but as I watched her take off, I felt as if my very last resource in the whole world, my last and only friend, was rolling out of my life.

7

To say that I was depressed as I rode up in the elevator of my apartment building would be an understatement. Actually, I was trying to convince myself that I was merely in a *recession*, not a full-blown depression. "All things must pass," I told myself, calling up George Harrison's lyrics from my favorite golden-oldies station, for a glimmer of hope. "The darkest hour is just before dawn," I then tried, thinking of The Mamas and The Papas. I even found myself resorting to, "It's up to you to do the ha-cha-cha."

I was trying to cheer myself up, but all I was doing was reminding myself that it was music that was responsible for this whole mess in the first place. If I hadn't struck up a friendship with Saul on the convenient pretext of writing a song for the WROX contest, he and Rachel never would have met. Then, I'd be flitting through a beautiful autumn Saturday morning—minus a broken heart and still aligned with my best friend—instead of drooping like an unwatered plant.

My morose mood was making me philosophical. I started thinking about the inevitable conflict between art and real life. Now, I don't generally go in much for this sort of deep thinking, especially while riding in elevators, but all of a sudden I could see nothing but complications. I had always expected to keep the two completely separate: I would have my creative work, and I would have my friends. And now things didn't seem quite as clear-cut. One was interfering with the other. As I let myself into the living room, I sighed so deeply and so loudly that my mother wandered in from her bedroom to see what was up.

"What's the matter, Sallie?" she said, her voice cheerful but her face taut with concern. "You sound as if you're carrying all the world's burdens on your shoulders."

"I feel that way. Why is it that everything always happens at once?"

"Maybe you'd like to talk about it."

I shook my head. "Thanks, but I think I'd just like to be alone for a while." I started for my bedroom, then realized that shutting myself up within those four white walls would drive me crazy. I paused in the living room for a second, then said, "On second thought, Mom, I'm going out for a couple of hours."

"Will you be back for lunch?"

"No, I don't think so. I'm going to the Museum of Natural History. Maybe staring at the dinosaur bones will make me realize how insignificant my problems are in the course of the world's history. Looking at something that's millions of years old always helps me put things back into perspective."

The American Museum of Natural History is one of my favorite places in the world. Once, when I was just a little kid, like five or six, my family came down to New York from Boston for the weekend. I remember that Jenny was still so tiny that my father had to carry her the whole time. Anyway, we went to that museum, and there were two things there that I never forgot. One was this huge whale, hanging from the ceiling. It's a real whale, too, or at least it used to be before it became an exhibit. It was so big that I spent years wondering how they ever got it inside the museum. I still haven't figured it out.

The other thing that left a lasting impression was the dinosaur bones. They have all these cavernous rooms at the museum, filled with the reconstructed skeletons of a tyrannosaur and a stegosaur and a couple of other kinds of dinosaurs. When I first saw them, I was awed by their size. You've got to remember that I was also a lot smaller then, too. But since then, the thing that really kills me about those guys is how old they are. I mean, we're talking millions and millions of years old here.

You stand in front of these dinosaurs, and you just think about what the world was like back then, when these things were tromping around New York City and France and everywhere else you can imagine, and you try to comprehend the idea of many millions of years. Doing that never fails to have this incredible effect on me. I start feeling really insignificant, but in an eerie kind of way. Stupid things like chemistry tests and freckles and fights with your best friend don't seem so overwhelming anymore.

So I hopped onto the Seventy-ninth Street crosstown bus, and within half an hour, I was standing in front of my old friends. In their usual manner, they proved quite helpful in banishing my vile mood. I stood there, just thinking about time and the world and life in general. I also watched the other people who filed through that room: couples holding hands, college students clutching spiral notebooks and looking serious, families with little kids.

There was one little girl who reminded me of myself. She was about five or six, and she really freaked out over my dinosaurs. In fact, she put up such a fight when her parents tried to drag her away from them that her mother had to promise to get her a book with pictures of dinosaurs from the museum store before she would consent to leave without screaming. I smiled at the little girl when they finally left. After all, she was one of us.

It must have been for almost an hour that I hung around the dinosaur exhibit. I started getting hungry, and I was just about to go out to Columbus Avenue in search of some makeshift lunch when I saw a familiar figure looming in the doorway. It was Saul. I could barely make him out through the giant ribs of Tyrannosaurus Rex. Suddenly, I was snapped back into the present again.

"Sallie! There you are! I called your house, and your mother told me I'd probably find you here." He ran toward me, a huge smile lighting up his face. His eyes were positively sparkling. He looked the way I had looked the week before, when I was convinced that I was in love. That realization alarmed me.

"Hi, Saul. What's up? Something major must have happened for you to have trekked all the way over here to find me." It was odd the way all of New York seemed to be seeking out my company all of a sudden. First Rachel, at Carl Schurz Park, and now, mere hours later, Saul, at the Museum of Natural History. I felt like the mayor.

"'Something major,'" he teased. "Yeah, I guess you could say so. Sallie, I've met the girl of my dreams!"

My heart sank into my stomach. I found myself feeling stifled by the air in the museum. It was as if no one had opened a window for millions of years, ever since Mr. T. Rex had wandered in and posed dramatically, in the hopes of one day becoming a permanent exhibit.

"And who, pray tell, might that be?" I had decided that playing innocent would be the safest route to take.

"As if you don't already know." Saul grinned. "None other than our Rachel Glass, your best friend and, hopefully, mine. She's great, Sallie. We had a wonderful time last night. I'd given up on meeting someone as terrific as Rachel. I think this could be it!''

At this point, a philosophical question comes to mind: Did I owe it to Saul to warn him? Or was it best to remain uninvolved? I don't know which would have been more ethical. But I do know which one I opted for. I took the coward's way out.

"That's nice," I said, smiling blandly.

"In fact," he went on, dragging me away from the dinosaurs, "I'm going to invite both of you, my two favorite ladies, to a musical performance tonight. I wanted to check with you first; are you free this evening?"

I nodded dumbly, allowing myself to be maneuvered through the museum.

"Good. Because I'm playing the guitar and singing at a retirement home out in Queens, and I'd like you both to be there."

"What do you mean?"

"Oh, it's just something I do sometimes on the week-ends. There's this place in Queens where a lot of older people live, and I go out and give them a little concert every now and then. It seems to cheer them up, and it's a lot of fun for me. There are about thirty women madly in love with me. And I'm in love with them, too. Of course, their average age is probably seventy-five, but no matter."

"How did this get started?" We were standing in front of a wall full of pay phones at that point, and Saul was rummaging through his pockets.

"A friend of mine used to work there part-time, and one Saturday night I had nothing to do so I went up to keep him company. I brought my guitar, as usual. And the next thing I knew, I was singing for a roomful of geriatric groupies. I loved the attention, and so I got hooked. Now I go out there whenever I can"—he put a quarter into one of the phones—"and tonight, I'd like you and Rachel to be my guests."

I opened my mouth, unsure of what exactly I intended to say, but Saul had already turned his attention to the invisible person he was talking to.

"Hello, Rachel? Hi! It's Saul."

I could hear a buzzing sound, like bees, as the indiscernible voice at the other end of the wire spoke.

"Fine. How about you? Good."

Saul glanced at me and gave me a wink. Once again, my heart had become disjointed and had relocated somewhere under my rib cage. I braced myself.

"So, listen, Rachel, I thought if you weren't doing anything tonight, maybe we could get together. I'm inviting you and Sallie to a kind of a concert."

I couldn't stand it anymore. I knew what was coming, and I could see no reason why I should have to witness it. I turned away and wandered into the gift shop nearby. As I distractedly fingered handwoven wall hangings from Guatemala and plastic models of birds of the great Northwest, I watched Saul's face through the glass that blocked out his voice. It didn't matter that I couldn't hear his words. His face told me that things were going exactly as I had anticipated.

When he finally hung up, I turned my back on him, pretending to be absorbed in a table full of books. I noticed that the little girl who loved dinosaurs was there with her parents, picking out a picture book on the world in prehistoric times. Even that failed to cheer me up.

I started when I felt a hand on my shoulder. I looked up into Saul's face and saw a big smile plastered on his face. It was almost convincing. *Almost*. Even in the bluish fluorescent light of the museum gift shop, I could see real pain in his cloudy dark eyes.

"Well, Sallie, it looks as if it won't be the three of us going out to Queens tonight after all. Rachel won't be joining us. But you're still invited, of course, if you'd like to come anyway."

I shook my head slowly. "I don't think so." I felt like some twentieth-century Judas.

"You knew, didn't you?" Saul said those words so offhandedly that I couldn't tell how hurt—or how surprised—he really was.

"Well . . . yeah, I guess. I—I talked to Rachel this morning, and . . ."

"What exactly did she say to you?" He was walking out of the museum so quickly that I practically had to run to keep up with him.

I hesitated. "She said that she liked you a lot, but that it bothered her that you two came from such different worlds."

"Translation: She can't hack the fact that I'm Puerto Rican."

"Saul, it's not her fault! It's her parents. They're the ones who are making all this so hard on her. They've always stressed the importance of appreciating her heritage, and so it's bound to influence her. Gee, ever since I met Rachel, she's only gone out with Jewish boys. Guys who come from a background that's identical to her own."

"In other words, you're saying that it's her problem, not mine."

"Well, of course! I mean, she likes you. A lot. And I think that's making all this even harder for her."

"Is that supposed to make me feel better?" Saul demanded, expressing anger for the first time. "I'm sorry, Sallie. I don't mean to take this out on you. You just happen to have the bad luck to be with me right now. Look, it's past one o'clock already. Have you had lunch yet?"

"No, but I'm not really very hungry." I wasn't. All this emotional stuff had managed to take my appetite away. I felt too full of other people's problems to find much room for food.

"Good. I'm too edgy to sit down anywhere. Here, how about a hot dog?" By that time, we were out on the street, and he gestured toward a man with a Sabrett frankfurter stand, planted near one of the entrances to Central Park. I nodded, and we sidled over and got ourselves a couple of franks and some cans of soda. Then we headed east across the park, back toward my neighborhood.

"I guess I just don't understand." Saul sighed, biting into his hot dog. "It's not easy to find people who are on the same wave length as you are. And I could tell right away that Rachel and I were right for each other. Sallie, haven't you ever felt that way about someone you just met? You just *knew* that the two of you were perfect for each other?"

"Um-hmm," I agreed enthusiastically, my mouth full of Diet Pepsi. That proved to be a mistake, because I could feel the tiny carbonation bubbles rising into my nose. The next thing you know, yours truly was choking to death right in the middle of Central Park, coughing uncontrollably and spitting out soda all over the sidewalk. Talk about conducting yourself with reserve and dignity.

"Now take somebody like you," Saul continued, patting me on the back. He never missed a beat as he went on with his monologue. "You're a mature, independent young woman, right?"

I nodded, hoping that my cheeks were not too red and that there was no Diet Pepsi dribbling down the side of my face.

"And your background is similar to Rachel's. Middle-class, Upper East side, charge accounts at Bloomingdale's?"

"You make it sound so bland and predictable," I protested, having reclaimed my reserve once again.

"You know what I mean." He paused while he finished

his hot dog. "You two are not that different in terms of your attitudes. So let me ask you: how would you have reacted if I had asked *you* out for last night, instead of Rachel?"

I buried my nose in my Diet Pepsi can, wishing I could climb inside. Since that seemed impossible, I instead adopted a restrained, lofty tone.

"Well, I guess I would have been happy about it. . . ."

"Let me rephrase that, and make it more general: how would *you* feel about going out with a Puerto Rican?'

I thought of my first reaction to Saul when I met him, then the defensive way I told my parents about him and the concerns I had over whether or not Rachel would approve of him. I had to admit that I had had to face the same kinds of things that Rachel was grappling with. Or, more accurately, the things she had chosen to *avoid* having to grapple with.

"It's funny, Saul," I said, giving his questions a lot of thought. "Those two questions seem entirely different to me. The idea of going out with some faceless, nameless creature who's identified solely as a Puerto Rican is a lot different from the idea of going out with *you*, Saul Rodriguez. Remember what you said to me that first night you came over? That everyone has stereotyped images of everybody else? Well, there's a lot of truth to that. 'Going out with a Puerto Rican' sounds rebellious, and daring, and a bit exotic. But then there's the reality of *you*. There's good old Saul, who likes music and tickling people and hot dogs with mustard, and looks like a cross between Cat Stevens and a teddy bear."

I sighed, suddenly feeling tired and extremely disgusted with the world in general. "I can understand Rachel's way of thinking. As much as I hate to admit it, you two *are* from very different backgrounds, and the one she's from places a whole lot of emphasis on preserving traditions and a certain kind of life-style and all kinds of stuff like that. And you, with your background, happen to be inconsistent with it."

"I see." Saul sounded sullen as he tossed his empty soda can into a trash bucket.

"You hate me now, don't you?"

"No, Sallie, I don't hate you. I understand what you're saying. Maybe I even agree that you're right."

"Well, it's odd that you should say that, because *I* don't think I'm right." I was surprised at how angry I sounded all of a sudden. I guess Saul was, too. "I understand where Rachel's coming from; I really do. But I don't understand why she can't see beyond her way of thinking, especially in this particular instance. I mean, you're a terrific guy, Saul! They don't make 'em any better than you! And Rachel knows that. I'm positive she does. So I think she's making a terrible mistake by letting you slip through her fingers like this."

"Thanks, Sallie. I appreciate your saying that."

"But I *mean* it, Saul." I stopped walking and looked at him earnestly. "Rachel and I always agree on everything. Or at least we always have in the past. That's been a major part of the foundation of our friendship. I know she'll always side with me, and I always support her in her decisions. But this time I think she's making a big mistake. And if she expects me to back her up, to tell her that I think she's doing the right thing . . . well, I simply can't do it. I sincerely think that Rachel is wrong."

At that point Saul leaned over and gave me a kiss on the cheek. It was just a little one, not mushy or theatrical or anything like that. I guess it was just his way of saying 'thank you.' I blinked hard and looked at him closely, and I could see that same lingering pain I'd first noticed at the museum gift shop.

"I'm glad you're my friend, Sallie," he said. "I'm sorry that I can't promise that one day you and I will walk into the sunset together, hand in hand, and live happily ever after, but I just don't see things happening that way." He paused. "Now, do you hate me?"

"No, not at all." I laughed. "I'm glad you're my friend, too. Not to mention my business partner."

"Oh, yeah. I'd forgotten about that." We were out of the park by then, standing on Fifth Avenue and watching the cars whiz by. "I had originally planned to spend today working on that song with you, but I'm afraid I don't feel much like doing it anymore. Do you mind?"

"Not at all."

"I think maybe I'll go home and work on it alone. It might make me feel better if I can get my mind off this whole thing."

"Okay." We continued walking together toward Lexington Avenue, where Saul could get the subway. Our conversation turned to our song and to the WROX contest, which was only one week away. The following Saturday night was the first level of the competition, and the truth was that I was getting nervous. Saul's social life was getting in the way of our progress as a creative team. "But we have to get together this week," I insisted as we neared the Eighty-sixth Street station. "We can't enter the contest unless we come up with those prize-winning lyrics."

"I know. And I'll be working on them. You do the same. I'll call you, Sallie!" he promised as he disappeared down the subway station steps.

I must admit, I was kind of relieved to see him go. I felt completely drained by the heart-wrenching day I had just lived through. First Rachel, that morning. And then the afternoon with Saul. I think the afternoon was even more difficult for me. There's one thing I'm completely convinced of, though: It's no easy thing, strolling through Central Park with a teddy bear who looks as if he's about to cry.

8

The thing I like best about New York City is its unpredictability. The very feeling of the place is unique. I honestly believe that if I were blindfolded and flown around in a helicopter for hours, then dropped anywhere in Manhattan, still blindfolded, I would be able to tell that I was in New York. Everything about it is just so *different* from anyplace else in the world that it simply cannot be compared to any other city.

For example, once I was standing in front of F.A.O. Schwarz, the giant toy store on the corner of Fifth Avenue and Fifty-eighth Street. Now, F.A.O. Schwarz is not just *any* toy store; it has all manner of wild and exotic paraphernalia that you simply cannot find anywhere else. It has twelve-room Victorian dollhouses, complete with tiny grand pianos and teensy-weensy forks and candlesticks; stuffed gorillas and lions and giraffes that are as big as the real ones that live in the Bronx Zoo; intricate marionettes with faces so lifelike that you expect them to start talking to you. The place is a total fantasy world, a little Disneyland right in the middle of midtown.

Anyway, on this particular occasion, there was a little girl standing near the entrance to the store, cradling a doll in her arms. This was not your usual doll; it was a male, for one thing, and it was dressed in some sort of uniform.

I leaned over and asked, "What's your doll's name?"

"He doesn't have a name," the little girl replied congenially.

"Well, I see he's wearing a uniform. Is he a policeman, or a soldier?"

"No," she answered, very matter-of-factly. "He's a doorman."

Only in New York. That's exactly the kind of thing that makes me giddy over the fact that I live here in this city that is as much of a fantasy land as F.A.O. Schwarz, only with real people instead of wooden and plastic ones.

As I walked home on that Saturday afternoon, after having watched Saul vanish into the New York subway system, I witnessed two things that had the result of changing my perspective on the whole situation. I was trudging along Eighty-sixth Street, lost in my own thoughts as I passed colorful fruit-and-vegetable stands and quaint German restaurants and bakeries. And all of a sudden a bum who was lurking in a doorway caught my eye. He was just your typical bum: dusty worn-out shoes, unshaven face, stringy black hair streaked with gray. But he was also wearing a brand-new, bright yellow sweatshirt with the name "Bennetton" printed across the front in bold black letters. Can you picture that? Needless to say, I couldn't help chuckling over that one.

Then, further down the street, I came across a panhandler begging for money. Once again, this is hardly a rare sight at the major crossroads of the city. But instead of the traditional tin cup, this particular guy was clutching a *paper* cup. You know, one of those waxy white ones with the purple and orange swirls printed on it. It was terrific.

Seeing things like this, commonplace occurrences with some unusual, unexpected twist, is hardly a rarity in New

York. But these two little events, superimposed over the terrible mood I had sunken into, managed to bring me back to reality. It was similar to looking at the dinosaur bones: In light of the world at large, my own situation began to look quite different from the time when I could see no farther than my own freckled nose.

I began to feel more hopeful, more determined to play an active part in setting things right instead of just sitting around watching everybody—myself included—go from feeling bad to feeling even worse. And so, as difficult as it would be, I resolved to confront Rachel and see if I could convince her that she was making a grave mistake. She was hurting Saul, she was hurting me, and, ultimately, she was hurting herself.

Once I had decided upon my strategy, I felt a sense of relief. After all, this was really the only thing to do. But at that point I was so wrung out by the emotionally grueling day that all I wanted was some time to myself. By the time I reached my front door, I had planned my schedule for the next twenty-four hours. It included, among other things, a very hot bath, an hour or so with my guitar, and an evening of goofing off with my sister, assuming she was amenable to the idea. Then, after I had basked in the luxury of these few indulgences, I would tackle the Saul-and-Rachel issue with full force.

That evening my parents went off to a party at the home of some friends of theirs who live up in Westchester County. Jenny and I had the apartment all to ourselves. It was great fun, carrying on like crazies instead of mature, responsible members of the Spooner household. We played our favorite records so loudly that they could be heard all over the apartment, stayed up late and watched a stupid but engrossing Sandra Dee movie on Channel 9, made popcorn and smothered it with more salt and hot melted butter than is generally deemed normal or even desirable by human standards. I discussed my plan with Jenny at great length, and she agreed that sitting down with Rachel and having it out was the best way—the *only* way to handle the whole situation.

So, the next day, Sunday, I set out for the Glass residence immediately after lunch. I must admit, however, that it was not entirely without trepidation that I tripped across the sidewalks toward East Seventy-seventh Street. I talk big, but when the heat is on, I am as much a victim of butterfly stomach and shaky knees as the next guy. It's not easy, telling your best friend that you think she's wrong, and that you've even gone so far as to side against her. I can honestly say that my allegiance was with Saul as I nodded to the doorman of Rachel's building and rode up the elevator. And being aware of that only contributed to my nervousness.

Feeling anxiety and approaching the Glasses' apartment are two totally incongruous actions. Just as I consider Rachel my sister, and Mrs. Glass my second mother, when I'm in the presence of Rachel's whole family—her parents plus her older brother, Steven—I feel as comfortable as when I'm with the Spooner clan. Perhaps even a bit *more* comfortable sometimes, because I know that certain topics of conversation, such as grades, noise level, and long red hairs in the bathroom drains, won't ever come up. Nevertheless, I was feeling true anxiety as I waited for the front door of the Glasses' apartment to be opened in response to my less-than-assertive knock.

It was Mrs. Glass who answered. Her face broke into a warm smile when she saw who it was, and a wave of relief rushed over me. It was a wonderful feeling, knowing that I was so welcome.

"Well, hi, Sallie!" she exclaimed. "What a nice surprise! Come on in!"

One of the best things about Mrs. Glass is that she always treats me as if I'm an equal when I pop over, as if I were visiting her or the whole family instead of just her daughter. I mean, the mothers of some of my friends always seem in such a hurry to push me off on their kids whenever I call or drop by. The instant they see me or recognize my voice on the phone, they say, "Oh, wait, I'll go get Jane," or whomever, and they dash off. Not Mrs. Glass. She and I have spent many an hour talking, discussing life, seated together at the kitchen table or on the living room couch. Sometimes, when I stop in and Rachel turns out not to be home, I end up visiting with her mother instead.

"It's been a while since I've seen you, Sallie," Mrs. Glass went on, leading me into the kitchen. "It's been at least two weeks. Has school been keeping you busy?"

It's funny—from the back, Mrs. Glass looks almost identical to her daughter Rachel. They're about the same size and build, and they both have shoulder-length black hair. Usually, Mrs. Glass wears her hair back in a ponytail—especially when she goes to work—but on this particular day, it was loose. With her wine-colored pants and pink cotton blouse, she was a ringer for Rachel.

"Yes, I guess I have been busy lately," I answered. I could tell by her voice that she had absolutely no inkling of what had transpired between Rachel and me during the last couple of days. It was better that way, too; while I can see real value in asking the opinions of people you trust, I've never been one to go dragging everybody and his uncle into my personal affairs. Apparently, that was true of Rachel as well.

"I was just going to have a cup of tea. Care to join me?" Mrs. Glass offered. "Here, I've got some cookies from that new French bakery around the corner. Let's have some while you tell me all about the courses you're taking this semester."

I sat down at the kitchen table, greedily digging into the package of cookies, whose two main ingredients were butter and chocolate. While the water boiled in a fire-engine-red enamel kettle, Mrs. Glass joined me. I gave her a quick rundown of all my classes.

"So you and Rachel aren't in any classes together this year?" She frowned when I had filled her in on my new schedule. "Now, that's too bad." She poured boiling water into two cups and handed one to me so I could dunk my own teabag. It was Earl Grey tea, as I recall.

"Yes, it is too bad," I agreed. "We hardly get to see each other anymore, since we've both been so busy with homework and exams and all that." I peered at her through the rising steam of my cup. "How *is* Rachel, anyway?"

"Oh, she's just fine. She's holed up in her room right now, working on some project for Spanish. A paper on *Don Quixote,* I think."

Just about then, Rachel's older brother, Steve, walked in. The most notable thing about Steven Glass is the fact that he was my very first major crush after I moved to New York. Soon after Rachel and I became friends and I started spending a lot of time at her house, I had the pleasure of meeting him.

He was a sophomore at Columbia University then, and I spent hours concocting fantasies in which he would invite me to some terribly exciting Christmas dance or something and fall madly in love with me. I think those fantasies included us moving into an apartment in Greenwich Village together, although why a student at Columbia would want to move all the way down to the opposite end of Manhattan is now completely beyond me.

Besides, I think that whole infatuation only lasted about a week. Once I saw that Steve was very big brotherish—which included teasing Rachel mercilessly and treating both of us as if we were mere *children*, simply because he had the status of being a worldly college student—he dropped from being Mr. Right back down to earthly status. And after he became Rachel's brother again, he and I began feeling pretty comfortable with each other. Sometimes he was even sort of protective of me, which had a certain charm about it.

Anyway, he came bounding into the kitchen with his usual unbridled energy. "Hi ya, Sallie!" he cried when he noticed me in the corner. "Long time, no see. Rachel's in her room. Hey, cookies! Where's Dad?"

I have long wondered if one of the skills taught at Columbia University is that of speaking in non sequiturs. Whether it's an official part of the curriculum or not, it certainly characterized the speech pattern of Steven Glass. Maybe it just emerged because he was always rushing off to someplace or other, so he never had time to light on any one subject. That day was no exception.

"I have to run, Mom. Got to hit the library. Oh, great, chocolate inside. Good to see you, Sallie." He grabbed a fistful of cookies, then disappeared as quickly as he had arrived.

"It's nice that Steve doesn't put on any airs around me," I commented. "It makes me feel even more like one of the family."

"Well, I'm glad you see it that way!" Mrs. Glass laughed.

"How are *you* doing, anyway?" I asked, suddenly aware that I had been so busy babbling on and on about myself that I had neglected to ask her anything about herself. "How's work?"

"Oh, it's fine. I've been busy, as usual, but I prefer it that way. I've been running around like a whirling dervish the past few weeks."

Mrs. Glass is an editor on the staff of a magazine for art dealers. It's rather specialized—not the kind of thing you curl up with in front of a fireplace and read cover to cover— but I've always been very impressed with the copies I've seen lying around the Glasses' apartment. It's printed on that thick, glossy paper, and it always has pages and pages of beautiful photographs of paintings in full color.

"That's good. And how is Dr. Glass?"

"Oh, fine. He's busy reading medical journals, I think. In

fact, I'm glad you stopped over, Sallie. It seems as if everybody is off by himself today, wrapped up in some project or other. It's nice to have someone to talk to. Would you like some more tea?"

"Thanks, I'd love some." I watched silently as she refilled my cup with hot water. "Mrs. Glass, is it okay if I ask you a really strange, off-the-wall question?"

"Of course, Sallie. What is it?"

I hesitated, then decided to come right to the point. "Okay, here goes. What exactly does being Jewish mean to you?"

"Hmm. That's not an easy question to answer," she replied, her face reflecting the serious consideration she was giving my question. "I suppose the one thing that most people who aren't Jewish have the most difficulty understanding is that it's more than a religion. It's an entire tradition, Sallie, a whole way of life. I feel that there's a very strong need to preserve the heritage, to remember the history, of the Jewish people."

"I guess that's mainly because of so much discrimination, especially in the past."

"Yes, that's true," she agreed. "In many countries, Jews weren't even considered citizens, even though they had been born there and lived there all their lives. And even now, in this so-called enlightened age . . . well, look at the oppression of Jews in places like Russia." Mrs. Glass shook her head slowly, then took a sip from her teacup. "We make a special effort to keep our heritage alive in order to prevent things like that from spreading, to keep history from repeating itself. I think that every ethnic group and every religion has some sense of its history, but to us Jews, it's especially important. I've made a point of educating Rachel and Steve about that heritage, and I know that they'll teach their children, too."

"What about the idea of Jews not marrying non-Jews?" I

ventured. "All those jokes about finding a 'nice Jewish boy'?"

"That's just one more aspect of preserving the Jewish tradition, Sallie."

"But isn't that limiting? I mean, I've gone out with boys of every religion and nationality you can imagine."

"I have never cut myself off from anyone because of religion or background or anything else. At least, I hope not." Mrs. Glass frowned. "But when it comes to marriage and having children and raising those children . . . well, that's a different story, and that's what's so difficult to explain. That's where those ties to the Jewish heritage come in. That sense of common understanding, of shared experience. And then there's an element of bonding as well. But then, again, that's true of most ethnic and religious groups, isn't it? Catholics are encouraged to marry other Catholics, and Italians are encouraged to marry other Italians. That idea just happens to be very strong in the Jewish religion." She bit into a cookie thoughtfully. "Am I explaining this in a way that makes sense to you?"

"Yes, I think so. And I guess Rachel feels pretty much the same way."

"Well, as I said before, I've always felt it was important to teach my children what being Jewish means. I think Rachel feels those same ties to Judaism, and that sense of importance about preserving her beliefs and her heritage."

"Hmm," I said, lost in my own thoughts. "That answers my question, then. Thank you."

"Glad to be of help. Can I offer you some more tea? Or another cookie?"

"No, thanks. I really came over because I have something important to discuss with Rachel."

Now another terrific thing about Mrs. Glass is that she never pries. She's the kind of person who accepts the fact that everybody has secrets, and she just leaves it at that. So instead of acting nosy or looking upset, she just said,

"Well, in that case, I'll leave you two to each other." She sighed and rose from the table. "It's just as well, because I should be proofreading an article on the rising costs of renting gallery space instead of wiling away the afternoon chatting and stuffing myself with cookies."

I followed her example and stood up. It was time, I knew; there was no more putting off what I had set out to do. I bid farewell to Mrs. Glass and the safety of the kitchen, and made my way through the apartment to Rachel's room. Without hesitating I knocked in the door and stuck my head in when her voice called, "Come in!"

Rachel was sitting at her desk, pen poised in midair over a tablet of white paper, eyes glazed from having been absorbed in some world other than our own. When she saw that it was me, her expression changed from blank to gleeful to serious, all in the matter of about two seconds. I could tell exactly what ran through her mind: first came the joy of recognizing a familiar, friendly face; second came the jolt of remembering that she was mad at me.

"Hi, Rachel," I said cautiously, bracing myself against possible attack, verbal or otherwise. "Are you busy?"

"Um, no. I guess not," Rachel replied in a stilted voice. "I'm working on this paper for Spanish, but it can wait. It's not due for a couple of weeks."

"Don Quixote?"

Rachel nodded. She continued staring at me as if she expected me to start tap-dancing or something. Instead, I moved awkwardly about her tiny bedroom, picking up various items, examining them, and putting them down again. Finally, when I could tolerate the silence no longer, I said, "Rachel, we have to talk. There's still a lot that needs to be said."

I have to confess, I had memorized that opening. I tried to make it sound spontaneous, and I think I even succeeded. But the truth was, I had already gone over this scene a hundred times in my mind. And that always seemed like the best way to begin. Nothing harsh, nothing judgmental. Simply an invitation for discussion.

"Okay," she said in that same strained voice. She put down her pen and turned her body around so she faced me. I sat on the edge of her bed and folded my hands in my lap.

"I—I think you know what it is I'm here to talk to you about."

"Well," Rachel said, "it could be one of two things, actually. It could be my relationship with Saul, or it could be my relationship with you."

"You're right." I hadn't exactly thought of it that way, but I had to agree with her. "They *are* two separate issues, aren't they?"

"Before you start yelling at me, Sallie, can I say something first? Look, I'm really sorry about yesterday. It was stupid of me to blame anything at all on you. I should never have lit into you the way I did when we were at Carl Schurz Park. The idea of letting something like this come between us is ridiculous. Our friendship is much too important for that."

I broke into one of those Christmas-morning type grins. "I'm glad you feel that way, Rachel, because I do, too."

"However," she went on, "I don't think you have any right to interfere in my relationship with Saul. What would have happened if you introduced me to some guy and I refused to go out with him because—I don't know— because he was too immature or not smart enough?"

"But that's not true!" I interrupted. "Saul *is* mature, and he *is* smart. . . ."

"You're missing the point," Rachel said calmly. "The basic problem here is that you're my friend, and you're Saul's friend as well. And so, matching the two of us up seems like the most natural thing in the world."

"But there's more to it than that! You like Saul, and Saul likes you, and, Rachel, believe me, you're making a huge mistake."

"Sallie, I know you think the world of Saul. That's pretty obvious. And maybe he is terrific. But there are other factors that you simply cannot understand." I thought of the conversation I had had with Mrs. Glass just a few minutes earlier.

Rachel stood up, then joined me on the bed. "Can we just drop this whole thing now and get on with our friendship? After all, discussing it forever is not going to accomplish anything except getting both you and me more frustrated."

"Okay," I agreed. I know when I've been defeated. I had given it my best shot, but there was nothing I could do. Besides, I was pleased as punch, as they say, that my friendship with Rachel had been restored. "Well, you can't blame me for trying. I promise I won't ever mention it again. Oh, Rachel, I'm so glad we're friends again! You can't believe how much I missed you!"

"I missed you, too!"

We hugged each other, and I felt good for the first time in ages. I felt as if there was so much I needed to tell Rachel— the little things that had happened in school and with my family and with my songwriting over the past week—and the two of us ended up chattering away for the next three hours. Poor old Don Quixote got left by the wayside.

When Mrs. Glass popped her head in to invite me to stay for dinner, I remembered that I still had to write a hasty fugue that evening for Monday's music theory class, and I got ready to leave. I stood up after giving Rachel another quick hug, and said, "Today turned out to be a magnificent day. I really wish I could stay for dinner, but Mom is expecting me, and I have a bunch of stuff to do for tomorrow. But listen, next Saturday night is the WROX competition, and I'm having a little party Friday evening. Nothing fancy, just enough people to supply Saul and me with a small audience. We're going to perform the song; it's sort of a dress rehearsal. Can you come?"

"Of course!" Rachel cried. "I wouldn't miss it for the world!"

Then her face darkened, as if it had just registered that Saul would be there. I could see she was torn between her recently renewed friendship with me and her wish to avoid seeing Saul. Happily, however, friendship won out. "What time should I come over?"

"I'm telling everybody to come at eight, so why don't you come a little earlier?"

"Okay. I'll even bring some of my Show-Stopping Brownies."

Show-Stopping Brownies are Rachel's specialty, a scrumptious combination of chocolate chip cookie dough and a cream cheese mixture, layered in a pan and baked like a cake. There are people who have literally become addicted to those things. In fact, I happen to be one of them.

"That would be terrific. Of course, I may be too nervous to eat. . . ."

"Then you can save them for after the competition."

"Good idea! Then I can have both cookies *and* fame and fortune. Well, look, I'm sure I'll end up talking to you on the phone in a couple of hours. I'd better get going now. Bye, Rachel!"

"Bye. Hey, Sallie?"

"Yeah?"

"Thanks for coming over." Rachel grinned, a trifle sheepishly.

I skipped home that night, feeling like a million dollars. The evening air was brisk and energetic, electrified with the promise of frosty winter weather. Life was good, and I felt exhilarated. Even the fact that poor Saul was still out in the cold, tossed aside and forgotten like Don Quixote, ceased to be of importance, at least for the moment. All that mattered was one simple fact: Rachel and I were friends again!

9

I love giving parties. The best part is not even having them; it's spending days planning and making lists and shopping and rearranging furniture. And just when you're convinced that there's not enough time to get everything done, it's the night of the party and the whole thing just falls into place.

That week turned out to be a busy one. Besides the party, there was the matter of the song for the contest. I mean, the whole purpose of Friday night's gathering was to present the world with this remarkable new musical creation, and come Wednesday, there was still no creation to speak of. A state of chronic panic had set in.

"Saul," I whined over the phone after school, "I know we're both supposed to be working on our song, but I just can't seem to get inspired. I'm suffering from writer's block. Ple-ease, you've got to come over tonight so we can work on the song!"

"Relax," came Saul's steady voice over the wire. "Our song is done."

"It's finished? You mean you've written the lyrics

already?" I was torn between a great sense of relief and the chagrined realization that our brainchild had been completed without me. What had happened to our team spirit?

"Well, not exactly. It's still rough around the edges. It needs some more work."

"How much more?" I was starting to feel a bit better.

"I'll bet you and I, working together, could whip it into shape in a couple of hours. It definitely needs an outside opinion, though. I can't quite get it to fit together. It's crying out for your touch."

All of a sudden I felt important. "Well," I said benevolently, "how about coming over Friday, early in the evening? I've invited a few people over for that night so we could try our song out on them. We'll have a few hours before they show up, and we can work on the song then. Think that's enough time?"

"Yeah, that should do it. What time should I come?"

I remembered my instructions to Rachel about coming over a bit early. It was at that point that I realized I had not yet given up on playing matchmaker. My attempts may have been halfhearted, but they were nonetheless hopeful.

"People will be coming around eight, so how about six?"

"Fine."

"Let's see. That'll give us two hours . . . sounds okay to me, too. As a matter of fact, you could read me the words right now, and I can work on them until we get together."

"Good idea."

Well, believe me, if I had been impressed with Saul's musical creativity before, I was positively bowled over by the set of lyrics he proceeded to recite to me. They were terrific! Of course, they did need some polishing up, but my mind was already racing with ideas on how to finish the song off. By the time he was done, I was actually jumping up and down.

"Saul, we can't lose! I'm totally floored! They're terrific!

You're terrific! And listen, here's what we can do. In the first line . . ."

My excitement grew over the next few days because of two reasons: the fact that the contest was getting closer and closer with each minute the clock ticked away, and the fact that I was certain our magnificent song could not lose. It became increasingly difficult to function as a normal human being. Doing things like going to school and washing dishes seemed pointless and mundane. After all, fame and fortune were not only lurking around the corner, they were so close that I could almost touch them!

The rest of that week dragged on. And then—*finally*—it was Friday, dinner was done, the bowls of nacho chips and M&M's were arranged in strategic places around the living room. Saul was due at any minute. I was ready for anything and everything as I sat with my guitar on the couch, excited and nervous.

This whole thing had become so important to me that even my lavender corduroy overalls weren't good enough. No, I had splurged and spent all my Christmas savings—what little there was—to buy myself a new pair of khaki-colored pants expressly to wear at the party and the contest. The image I conveyed with those pants and a blue-and-white striped cotton blouse was dignified and serious. The effect was much more suitable for a professional songwriter than purple corduroy, I was certain.

Saul was on time, in his usual style, although at the sound of the doorbell I jumped about nine thousand feet. I had even lost the will to pair him off with Rachel; that's how involved I was in the WROX contest. Saul had become nothing more than my musical partner. My concerns about his social life were buried deep beneath my stage fright.

"Hi," he said calmly, waltzing in and tossing his jacket onto a chair. "How's our song?"

"Finished," I said, trying to sound triumphant but instead sounding scared. "At least I *think* it's finished."

"Sallie," Saul scolded me, "surely you're not *nervous*, are you? Look, we can't lose. You said so yourself. Tomorrow night you've got to get on that stage with the attitude that you're doing the audience a favor by letting them hear your song. You've got to start believing in yourself. And in *us*, as a team."

"I believe." My meek voice sounded anything but convincing. Saul sat down on the couch next to me.

"Okay, why don't you run through the song for me a couple of times so I can hear what you've done with it. Then we can work on our performance technique. I have an idea for an unusual harmony for that part at the beginning."

My family is well trained. They know when it's safe to deal with me, and when it's in their best interest to lie low. That evening, they must have sensed my anxiety and been keenly aware of how important the contest was to me, because they all managed to disappear. I discovered later that Dad had taken Jenny to a movie, while Mom, who had volunteered to play the role of unobtrusive chaperon, read in her bedroom with the door open and one ear cocked toward the living room. As far as the Spooners were concerned, the apartment was mine for the rest of the evening.

With no distractions from relatives, I became totally absorbed in our song. Saul and I ran through it a dozen times, and then I made him run through it another dozen. Not only were our entire futures at stake, but tonight all my friends would be judging the very first Spooner-Rodriguez endeavor. I was becoming more confident, however. My faith in myself and Saul and our song gradually replaced my doubts and my stage fright.

Time sped by. When the doorbell rang, I jerked my head up, surprised at being pulled back into reality.

"Is it eight o'clock already?" I gasped.

"No," Saul replied, glancing at his watch and looking a bit disconcerted. "It's only seven-thirty."

Then I remembered. "Oh, right, that must be Rachel."

"Rachel?" Now it was Saul's turn to look surprised.

"Oh, didn't I tell you? I asked her to come over a little early tonight. You know, to help out with the party. Gee, I still have to mix the onion dip, and fill the ice bucket. . . ."

Saul remained silent. He just plucked at his guitar and appeared to be uncomfortable. I felt kind of sorry that I hadn't given him any warning. The bell rang again, and I jumped up to answer the door.

"Hi, Sallie!" Rachel said breathlessly. She thrust a tin from Kjeldsen's Butter Cookies at me and explained, "Here. Show-Stopping Brownies. They're still warm. And I doubled the recipe, to make sure you'd have some left over."

Her face was flushed, as if she had run over to my house in the cool autumn evening, and her eyes were bright. Her attention was focused on the buttons of her coat. She fumbled with them as she strolled into the living room. When she finally looked up, she froze dead in her tracks.

"Oh, hi, Saul," she said, trying to sound casual.

"Hi, Rachel," he replied in a similar tone.

"I—I didn't realize you'd be here already."

"No, and Sallie didn't mention you'd be coming over early, either."

"Well," I said with forced cheerfulness, "since we now have a cast of thousands present, how about if you guys help me get ready? I still have a million things to do. Let's get started in the kitchen."

Saul, Rachel, and I made clumsy small talk as we went about doing odds and ends, those typical party things that have to be left for the last minute. Perhaps that half hour before the other guests started arriving was excruciating; I really have no idea. I was so wrapped up in myself once again that I was totally uninvolved with the rest of the world. This time, however, it was the role of hostess for the elite of New York City—or at least of our high school class—that was making me jittery. Stage fright had been put on hold for those few minutes I had to try and pull off a successful party. From what I can remember, however, Saul and Rachel were civil to each other. Not belligerent and not lovey-dovey, just two polite guests up to their elbows in sour cream.

At precisely 8:05, the doorbell rang. I squealed.

"That doorbell is going to drive me crazy before this evening is through! Mark my words: they'll be carting me away by 8:15. Well, hi there, Sharon! I'm glad you could make it! Here, let me take your sweater. I'll just put it in the bedroom. . . ."

I understand that it's considered chic to be "fashionably late" in some circles. Not in mine. Perhaps it's the lure of food, or maybe I just hang out with a dull crowd . . . I don't know. What I do know is that by 8:20, the living room was full and a party was in full swing.

Parties are like everything else in life that provokes apprehension or self-doubt: once they're under way, once you see how easy it is, it becomes simple. After I made certain everyone had a glass of something in one hand and a Show-Stopping Brownie in the other, I began to relax. I turned up the Madonna album that was playing on the stereo as my little group of friends got more relaxed and more boisterous.

I have to admit, the evening was turning out to be a success. Energy was high, and people did their best to mingle. Even I was having fun, a sure sign of a good party. I forgot to be nervous about the upcoming contest, or even the impending musical debut of our new song. I managed to devour eight—count 'em, *eight*—Show-Stoppers, proof that there were no butterflies taking up space inside my stomach.

"And you thought you'd be too nervous to eat," Rachel kidded me as she watched me stuff one of the heavenly little tidbits into my mouth.

I chewed, then swallowed. As soon as I could manage to sound like a human being once again, I said, "You know I'm your greatest fan. I know no limits as far as Show-Stoppers are concerned. Ooh, I love the cream cheese part. It tastes like ice cream."

"Sallie, is there any particular reason why you invited me over early tonight?" Rachel scrutinized me so closely that I started to squirm.

"Why, no. Oh, I see. You think I'm still trying to get you and Saul together. Well, you can rest easy. It was perfectly innocent, I assure you. I was after you for your dip-making abilities, not your girlish charms." I shrugged. "One cannot force matters of the heart, can one?"

"No, I guess one can't." Rachel munched on a handful of M&M's, then turned to me. "Hey, what about your song? It's almost 9:30 already. How much longer do we have to wait for the big preview?"

Instant butterflies. And here I thought I was managing to remain as cool as a cucumber. "Oh, yeah, I suppose you're right. Now is as good a time as any. Let me go find Saul."

I gulped, then made my way through the cluster of bodies in my living room, planted together in small groups or draped across the couch and chairs. I found Saul talking to Sharon, over in a corner.

"Excuse me, Sharon. Can I steal Saul away? I think it's show time."

"Oh, great!" Sharon cried. "I can't wait!"

Well, that's *one* fan, I told myself as I picked up my guitar and clinked a glass for silence.

"Hey, guys," I cried, having decided that "Attention!" was too formal for the occasion. "Listen, everybody. As most of you know, I had an ulterior motive in inviting you to this little soiree. Tomorrow night is the first level of the WROX Songwriting Competition. It will be held in our high school auditorium at eight o'clock, and I hope you'll all come.

"But you are among the lucky, for you have been chosen, out of all our fellow students, for a special preview. In case any of you haven't met him yet, this is Saul Rodriguez, my songwriter partner. We're entering the contest at my school because this whole crazy thing was my idea in the first place.

"Anyway, whether you can make it tomorrow night or not, Saul and I would like to run through the song once or twice for you. And then we'd like your honest opinions. Notice I stressed the word *honest*. This is no time to be polite or generous. Tonight is our last chance to make any changes, so we really want to know what you guys think.

"Ready?" I glanced over at Saul, who stood next to me at one end of the living room. He nodded, and then I surveyed the room briefly to make sure everyone else was all set. I saw two dozen faces gazing at me intently, *expectantly*. And then I had a terrific surprise: I wasn't nervous at all. I was excited, but I wasn't nervous. I was actually looking forward to sharing our wonderful song with my friends.

I got lost in the music as we sang. I concentrated so hard on making it sound good that the rest of the room just fell away. I had to admit, Saul and I sounded great as our voices tripped over the melody we had created, blending together,

sometimes in unison, sometimes in harmony. The lyrics
glided together to form a song:

If someone leaves me waiting on the corner for an hour,
Or forgets she left the milk out of the fridge and it turns
*   sour,*
Or forgets that it's my birthday or forgets to leave the
*   key,*
Or argues with the traffic cop when I'd rather let it be,

Then I start to feel
Maybe I was wrong;
That I'm spending too much time with her
And not enough with my simple songs.

Then I say
Maybe it should end.
But if that someone else is you—
Then it's okay.

If someone likes the city lights and I prefer the sea,
Or if when she looks into my eyes, she doesn't quite see
*   me,*
If she always has her steak well-done and I prefer it
*   rare,*
If she tries to hide or run away when I tell her that I
*   care,*

Then I start to feel
Maybe I was wrong;
That I'm spending too much time with her
And not enough with my simple songs.

Then I say
Maybe it should end.
But if that someone else is you—
Then it's okay.

If someone says she's crystal and that I am only glass,
That our two worlds are different and our love could
*   never last,*
"But both of them are fragile, they need tender care," I
*   claim,*
"And if both of them should shatter, then they both
*   would look the same,"*

Then I start to feel
Maybe I was wrong;
That I'm spending too much time with her
And not enough with my simple songs.

Then I say
Maybe it should end.
But if that someone else is you—
Then it's okay.

When we had finished, I stood before my friends for a few seconds without saying a word. I was just watching their faces. Sometimes you can tell a lot more by people's expressions than by the words they're saying. And what I saw was very satisfying. I saw looks of absorption, of appreciation, of surprise.

As I scanned the crowd, feeling smug, my eyes were drawn to one particular face in the crowd. Was it just a quirk of the lighting in the room, or were those actually tears in Rachel's eyes? I glanced over at Saul. Their gazes were locked together, just as they had been that first night they met.

How blind I had been! I can't believe now that up until that moment it hadn't even occurred to me that Saul had written the lyrics for Rachel! She had been his inspiration. And here I was, defending him right and left in her presence. Saul Rodriguez was apparently quite capable of taking care of himself.

There was a flurry of activity then as my friends gathered around us and showered us with compliments. Jenny's prediction was proving to be accurate: They loved "If That Someone Else Is You" in New York. It was a hit! Needless to say, I was ecstatic.

"I love it!" Sharon squealed. "You guys can't lose!"

"Did you two really write that?" Jane asked, wide-eyed. I had to laugh; she sounded just like me the night I met Saul.

I basked in the glory of success for a few more minutes, then turned back to Saul to ask him if he was as happy with the song as everyone else seemed to be. He was gone. I shrugged, assuming that if he had felt we needed to make any changes, he would have let me know. I concentrated all my efforts on enjoying the party once again.

By that point I couldn't wait for the competition. I was so exhilarated that I was convinced that Saul and I couldn't lose. "A star is born!" I kept telling myself. I was ready to take the music world by storm. I celebrated with two more Show-Stopping Brownies.

When I stepped into the kitchen to retrieve more ice cubes for my guests, I discovered my mother sitting at the kitchen table with a cup of tea.

"Oh, hi, Mom. I didn't realize you were in here. Have one of Rachel's brownies with your tea. They're terrific."

"Sallie, I heard your song just now. It was beautiful! I'm so proud of you!"

She gave me a hug. I found myself growing embarrassed.

"Well, it's just a little ditty Saul and I threw together."

"Don't be so modest! It's wonderful. And whether it wins tomorrow night or not, you should be proud of yourself. You've got a lot of talent."

"Thanks, Mom."

"Where is Saul? I'd like to congratulate him, too."

"Um, I think he stepped out for a minute. But I'll tell him what you said as soon as he comes back."

Just then, a bunch of people burst into the kitchen, clamoring for more ice. I was sort of glad; it's not easy, having people compliment you, especially when it's your own mother who's acting impressed. I realized I had to learn how to handle success. I would have to develop the gracious modesty of Jackie Kennedy Onassis if I was going to be thrust into the limelight all the time.

Around midnight, my friends started trickling out.

"Thanks for a great party, Sallie!"

"And good luck tomorrow!"

"Yeah, we'll be there, rooting for you!"

"Look for us in the front row!"

When I had shut the door after the last guest and began collecting empty paper cups from every flat surface in the room—including the floor, the piano, and the chessboard—I realized that I hadn't seen either Saul or Rachel after we had done the song. It struck me as odd, but it was hardly something to dwell on. Sooner or later, one of them would fill me in on what had happened.

For that moment, I couldn't get excited about Saul and Rachel. I was too happy about the promise of the next night's contest. I was counting on the thrill of victory. Never before had I felt so confident, so optimistic. As I crumpled up an armload of paper cups and thrust them into a huge plastic bag, the fluttering of my heart told me that all the waiting, all the plotting and planning, all the hours alone with my guitar were beginning to pay off. And from the way I was feeling, I had absolutely no doubt that it was all worth it. I suspect that never before had anyone who was knee-deep in dirty dishes and crumpled-up paper napkins and melting ice cubes felt so good.

10

Whenever I'm anticipating something that's out of the ordinary, I spend the entire night before having dreams about it. Or sometimes, nightmares. I remember the night before I started school in New York, back when we had first moved here. All night as I slept, a stream of terrifying, grotesque people paraded through the doors of an imaginary classroom, while I sat in the front row clutching my old book bag from Boston. There was one student clad entirely in black leather, and one dressed like a New York policeman, and a girl with bright red lipstick and platinum-blond hair and a silver-sequined evening gown. Of course, in the light of day, the whole thing seemed hilarious, and the fear I had associated with those bizarre characters faded quickly as I busied myself with real life.

The worst thing about that kind of dream is that you spend the whole night living through whatever it is you're dreading, and then you wake up to find that you haven't really done it at all, that it's still ahead of you. Maybe that's what they mean when they say, "A coward dies a thousand deaths, a brave man dies just once." At any rate, dreams have a way of telling you what it is you're really feeling about something. You can't fool yourself when you're asleep and all your defenses are down.

The night before the WROX songwriting contest was the perfect example. I went to bed excited—positively *gleeful*—over the prospect of the competition. And then all night I had horrible dreams in which everything that could possibly go wrong went wrong. Saul didn't show up; he showed up but forgot the song; I forgot the song; the audience turned into ducks, and we couldn't sing over the noise they were making. It was exhausting, and by the time I woke up, I was totally drained.

I had hoped to sleep late, to make sure I was still radiant and refreshed by eight o'clock that night. Instead, I found myself up and at 'em by seven. No one else was awake yet, and I lay in bed for a long time, thinking about the evening ahead. I also sang the song to myself, in my head, about eighty-three times.

When I heard someone walking around in the kitchen, I threw on a bathrobe and raced out of my bedroom, happy over the prospect of some company. It was Mom who was bustling about in the dawn's early light, making a pot of coffee and toasting English muffins.

"Good morning," she greeted me as I stood in the doorway, rubbing my eyes. "How's the songwriter today? All set for the contest?"

"Couldn't we talk about something else?" I pleaded as I put on the kettle to make myself a cup of tea.

"Don't tell me you're nervous! Not after you gave such a sterling performance last night! You've already done it once, so what's there to worry about?"

"Judges. An auditorium filled with people. A million other contestants. And the fleeting promise of fame and fortune. That's all."

"You'll do fine," Mom assured me. "Do you want us all there, or would it be easier for you if we stayed away?"

"No, you can come if you like." At that point it didn't matter at all to me. What were three more people when I would be singing to hundreds?

Just then Jenny's voice piped up, "You mean today is the day that our Sallie becomes a star, and all we have to offer her is English muffins? That will never do!" Enter Jenny, in her pink-and-white flowered nightgown and Deerfoam slippers. "I think hot cinnamon buns would be much more appropriate."

Jenny kissed me good-morning on the cheek, kissed my mother, then buried her head in the refrigerator. "I know we have some of those . . . oh, here they are!" She emerged with a roll of cinnamon-bun dough, looking triumphant. "Just give me twenty minutes, and the feast will be on."

"Who mentioned food?" my father said sleepily as he appeared in the doorway wrapped up in a red-plaid bathrobe. "If it's something Jenny is making, then I want a double order."

"Coffee's ready." Mom smiled.

It isn't often that the four Spooners get to sit down at the kitchen table and have breakfast together, like the families you always see on television. Everyone's schedule is so different, and everybody is always in such a hurry that it's almost like a party when we have time to spend as a family, drinking coffee and discussing our plans for the day.

"Well, Sallie," Dad said, "I understand you made quite a hit last night. Your mother assures me that you'll be winning first prize and that you will have bought a dozen white Rolls Royces by next week."

"She's in it for the artistic satisfaction, not the money," Jenny insisted. "Oh, and maybe for the fame part, too."

"I'm looking forward to tonight," he went on. "Is it okay if I bring my camera and take pictures?"

"Dadde-e-e!" Jenny squealed. "That's so unprofessional!"

"That's not necessarily true," Mom said. "There are always photographers at the Oscar and the Emmy Awards."

"Well, on one condition, then," Jenny said. "He'll have to wear a tuxedo."

I appreciated the fact that my whole family was being so supportive. They really are dears, every last one of them. By the time Jenny had taken her cinnamon buns out of the oven and the entire kitchen smelled scrumptious, I had managed to relax a bit. After all, how could this competition—or *any* competition—be scary when I had these three in the audience, cheering me on?

It was a pleasant way to start the day, lingering over two cups of tea and stuffing myself with hot rolls. I could have stayed forever, but as Jenny was just finishing her detailed description of the plot of the movie she and my father had seen the night before, the telephone rang.

"I'll get it." I assumed it would be Saul, checking up on some last-minute detail about the contest.

"Hello?"

"Hi, Sallie. It's me."

I had been expecting to hear Saul's deep voice, so I was surprised to be greeted by a female.

"Who . . . oh, Rachel, of course! Hi! I'm sorry. My mind is already on the stage of the auditorium. You'll have to bear with this absentmindedness I seem to have contracted."

"Sallie, I'm in love!"

"Congratulations! Who's the lucky fellow? Anyone I know?"

"Saul, of course."

Of course. A mere week before, I had been obsessed with getting Rachel to consider even going out with him, as if I were asking her to sell all her worldly goods and move to the Himalayas. And now she was saying, "I'm in love with Saul, of course."

"I think I missed something, Rach. You'd better fill me in."

"It happened last night," she began dreamily. "I don't know exactly how. I mean, I was kind of apprehensive about seeing Saul at your party, and at first it was awkward. We didn't really know what to say to each other, how to act toward each other. It was that way until he started to sing. Until you *two* started to sing," she corrected herself.

"Then, all of a sudden, I saw him differently. I fell in love with him on the spot. I guess it's partly because he seemed like some kind of celebrity or something, standing there performing for an audience. But it was more than that, too. It was the song. He had written that song for *me*. And it was so beautiful. The sentiment behind it was so sweet, so *sincere*."

"I worked on it, too," I interjected. I wasn't anxious to be demoted to the role of silent partner.

"Oh, I know. But I could tell that the emotion in the song was from him. Wasn't it?" she added uncertainly.

"Well, yes," I admitted. "He came up with the idea. I just refined it, made the words fit with the music better. Some of the lines were completely mine. But you're right: you definitely were the inspiration for that song."

"I hadn't realized he felt that way about me," Rachel went on. "I didn't know he cared that much!"

"For heaven's sake, Rachel! What do you think I've been trying to tell you? Well, at any rate, I'm glad you two worked it out. Hey, where did you guys disappear to, anyway?"

"We went out for a walk along the river. It was so lovely." She sighed. "We strolled through Carl Schurz Park and looked at the city lights. . . . It was very romantic."

"And then?"

"And then he kissed me."

"And *then*?"

"And then we walked up to Baskin-Robbins and had an ice cream cone."

"Rachel!" I groaned. "You're not much on details, are you?"

"Oh, I had one scoop of pumpkin pie and one of strawberry-banana, and he had—"

"That's not exactly what I meant!"

"Sallie!" Rachel sounded indignant. "A woman in love cannot be expected to bare her soul to anyone! Not even her best friend! I'm appalled that you're even asking!" And then she proceeded to fill me in on every detail of the entire evening.

"So, I didn't get home until two," she finished. "Fortunately no one had bothered to wait up for me. They all assumed I was snug and safe at your house."

"It sounds magnificent," I said. "And I'm so happy for you! And for Saul, too. Gee, I can't believe things are working out so well, and so easily!" Especially after I had put so much worrying into their relationship.

"Well, enough about me. How about you, Sallie? Are you excited about tonight? By the way, you were completely, totally, utterly fantastic last night."

"Thank you. Yeah, I guess I am excited about tonight. Nervous, too."

"You'll be great. And I'll be out there on the other side of the footlights, applauding my heart out for you. Believe me, the two of you can't lose."

"I think you're a bit prejudiced, but thanks for your confidence, just the same."

"Oh, by the way, Sallie, how about coming over to my house after the contest? I told my mother about it, and she invited you and Saul over for a celebration. Think you'll be up for it?"

I paused for a second to reflect on how I had felt the night before, after my performance. "Rachel, if it goes well tonight, I'm sure I'll be so euphoric that I'll be flying around the room for days. I'd love to come over tonight."

I didn't bother to mention that if it went poorly, I would probably be so devastated that I would need the love and support of Rachel and Saul and the Glass family and everybody else in the world who I felt was on my side. But there was no use in being pessimistic.

"Well, then, break a leg!" Rachel said cheerfully. "I'll see you tonight!"

As I hung up the phone, I felt kind of strange. I was happy for Rachel, and I was scared about the contest. Those two feelings were in direct conflict with each other, and it was confusing. I only had enough room for one set of feelings. The contest won. It was all I could concentrate on at that point. I would have to block everything else out and pour all my energy into getting psyched up for it.

The rest of the day passed in slow motion. I didn't quite know what to do with myself, so I ended up doing very little. I straightened up my room, washed my hair, listened to my favorite records for inspiration. My family left me alone, except to smile encouragingly whenever any of them passed me in the hall or ran into me in the kitchen.

Saul called in the afternoon, to make sure everything was all set. He didn't mention Rachel at all, which I took as a sign of the utmost professionalism. He gave me a pep talk, and we agreed to meet at the auditorium at 7:30.

When the hands of the clock pointed to six o'clock, a heavy feeling of dread descended upon me. Evening had officially begun. I was silent during dinner, and I ate so little that Jenny felt obligated to make a comment about how unusual my habits had become. Immediately after dinner I closed myself up in my room. I had an hour left before it was time to leave for the auditorium. An hour.

I dressed in my khaki pants and my striped shirt, fastened my hair back with tortoiseshell combs, applied enough makeup to look mature but not overdone. I tuned my guitar and ran through my song a few more times. With every movement, with every passing second, the knots in my stomach grew.

And then it was time. I could put it off no longer. Just as the deejay on WROX announced that it was seven-twenty, there was a knock at my bedroom door. It was Jenny.

"Are you about ready?" she asked lightly. "I'll walk you over to the auditorium. Mom and Dad will be over in about half an hour."

"Yeah, I'm ready." I gulped, then looked around my bedroom forlornly. The next time I see this room, I thought, I will be either euphoric or depressed. The next time I see this room, all this waiting will be over.

I pulled on a jacket and picked up my guitar as Jenny looked on. Her expression was sympathetic, as if she were feeling the same nervousness that I was. I was glad she was walking me over. Sometimes it helps to have someone to lean on, even if that someone is four inches shorter than you.

"Got everything?" she asked, and I glanced around the room one more time.

"Yeah, I think so." I inhaled deeply and clutched my guitar tightly. "This is it, Jenny. Let's go."

11

Things were already buzzing by the time Jenny and I showed up at the high school. The contest, with its promise of an appearance by one of the better-known disc jockeys from WROX, had brought my classmates out in droves. It was the social event of the season; the sidewalks, as well as the lobby outside the auditorium, were littered with the bodies of friends and strangers who hung out, meeting and greeting. As Jenny and I made our way through the scattered groups of kids, I spotted Dan Meyer flirting with a girl I recognized as a sophomore. He was so busy trying to impress her that he never even noticed me. My heart went out to her.

My old chemistry teacher, Ms. Storm, had the question-able honor of guarding the door to the backstage area. It was her job to keep out those who were merely curious spectators, allowing entry only to the privileged few.

"Well, hello there, Sallie. How have you been?" she greeted me. "And who have we here?"

"Hi, Ms. Storm. I'm fine. A bit nervous, but fine. This is my sister, Jenny."

"Hello, Jenny. Are you a contestant, Sallie?" Ms. Storm scanned the clipboard she was holding. "Oh, yes, here's your name. 'Sallie Spooner, with Saul Rodriguez.' You can go on backstage. All the contestants are in the band room."

As Jenny and I started through the doorway, she said, "Oh, I'm sorry, but your sister will have to stay outside. I have strict instructions to let in contestants only." She smiled apologetically. "That's a WROX rule."

"That's okay," Jenny assured her. "Sallie doesn't need me, anyway."

"Yes, I do!" Suddenly, I felt as if I couldn't go on without Jenny at my side.

"Relax, Sallie. Saul will be here any minute, if he's not already inside. You two will be so busy getting everything together that you'll never even miss me. Now go out there and knock 'em dead. Remember, we're all in the audience rooting for you!"

Blindly I found my way to the band room. The other hopefuls were spread out all over the place, warming up on harmonicas and flutes and other assorted, unlikely musical instruments. There were a few people tuning guitars, and there was a small crowd waiting their turn at the upright piano that was pushed against the wall. The air was electric with tension and excitement.

I staked out a corner of the room as my own and slowly took off my jacket and started tuning my guitar again, still surveying the room. There were some faces that I recognized, although most of the contestants were strangers. It seemed as if there were dozens of people packed in there, but I later found out that there were only fifteen songs entered in the contest.

When Saul walked in a trifle uncertainly, I instantly felt a million times better. A look of relief crossed his face, too, as he spotted me across the room.

"You made it!" I cried.

"Did you ever doubt it?" Seeing his grin reminded me that this was supposed to be fun, not some new form of torture. "And how is Ms. Spooner doing tonight?"

"Okay, I guess. I wish it were over already."

"Nonsense. The best part is yet to come. Once you've experienced the joy of being in the spotlight, the thrill of applause that's meant only for you, I'll never be able to drag you off the stage. Whether we win this thing or not, I expect us both to have the time of our lives."

I wished I could believe him. But before I had time to dwell on his prediction, my attention turned to a man who had stood up on a chair and was clapping his hands.

"All right, contestants, can I have your attention, please? My name is Al, and I'm from WROX, 'The radio station that really rocks.' Tonight I'll be making sure things go smoothly. Your emcee will be Rusty O'Shea, WROX's top disc jockey. Let's hear it for Rusty!"

An aging man with a pot belly waved energetically from the crowd, crying, "Hi ya, kids! It's great to be here!"

"I had no idea he was so *old*!" I whispered to Saul.

"I know," he agreed. "He sounds so young and enthusiastic on the radio. I thought he was about twenty years old!"

"Anyway," Al, who apparently had no last name, went on, "we'll be getting started in just a few minutes. I'd like to ask two things of each of you. One, please don't leave the band room. We don't want any of you getting lost just when it's time for you to go on. And two, please keep it down while someone is performing onstage. Sound has a way of traveling extremely well whenever you don't want it to. We don't want the audience to be distracted.

"Now, I'm going to call your names in the order you'll be going on. Please listen carefully, because we want to make sure things keep moving along out there. The last thing we need tonight is a restless audience. We're going to try to make this as professional as possible, and we know you'll all do your very best to help us out.

"Okay. The first ones to go will be Charlie MacDougal and Ellen Rubin. . . ."

Saul and I were on fourth. "That's good," he assured me. "That way the audience will be warmed up, but they won't be tired or bored yet."

"I just hope we can hear the other people," I said, suddenly worried about our competitors. Even though I was confident that our song was terrific, I had no idea what we would be competing against.

"Let's go stand over by the door. That way we should be able to hear what's going on onstage. They're using microphones, aren't they?"

"Microphones?" I repeated. "I—I've never used a microphone before."

"Nothing to it. You'll see."

I wanted to respond, but my throat was so dry that no words would come out. I wondered how Steve Martin and David Brenner and all those people feel while they're backstage, waiting to go on the Johnny Carson show. If this was so difficult, how could anybody ever hack Hollywood?

At a couple of minutes after eight o'clock, Rusty O'Shea burst out onto the stage, suddenly bubbling over with energy and personality. It was as if he was transformed by being the center of attention.

"Good evening, folks, and welcome to WROX's First Annual Songwriting Contest, here in the wonderful city of New York! As you probably know, this whole thing was put together by WROX, New York's leading rock station. Remember, WROX is the radio station that really rocks! I'm Rusty O'Shea, and I'll be your host for tonight. Now before we get started, I'd like to say . . ."

"I hope he doesn't go on for much longer," Saul said

softly. "It looks as if we may be losing Charlie and Ellen here."

I glanced over at the first two contestants, who were standing at the front of the informal little line we had all made near the door. It was true; Charlie looked as if he were about to pass out, and Ellen had twisted a pink tissue into shreds.

"You're right," I said. "I hope Ellen isn't planning to play the piano. Her fingers would probably slip right off the keys."

Seeing how nervous those two were managed to make me feel a little better. After all, we were all in this together, and somehow we would all get through it. And Saul was right: whether we won or not, we should try to have fun.

"And so here are our first contestants," called Rusty's familiar voice, "Charlie MacDougal and Ellen Rubin. Let's give Charlie and Ellen a warm welcome now. Come on!"

Charlie and Ellen shuffled onto the stage as if they were being sent into battle. Never before had I seen two more unhappy-looking people. I leaned forward expectantly, anxious to hear their song.

After a smattering of applause and the sound of a piano bench screeching across a wooden floor, there came a lovely introduction. Their song had the same kind of beat as ours, and I glanced at Saul nervously.

"It sounds like our song."

"No, it doesn't," he assured me. "Ours is better."

Actually, he was right. Once they got going, I had to agree that our song *was* better. Theirs had a good beat, but the words and even the melody just did not deliver. It was a disappointment, and audience reception was cool.

"No competition," Saul whispered, even though he applauded politely along with the invisible audience lurking beyond the dark maroon velvet curtains that kept us all tucked away out of sight.

"Thank you, Charlie and Ellen," Rusty O'Shea said when the two of them slunk back to where we were all waiting, Ellen red-faced and Charlie still looking as if he were about to pass out. "And now, three sophomores are going to do their song, 'Red, Yellow, Pink.' Let's hear it for Todd Williams, Tony Corona, and Jeff Nash."

A strange thing about Todd, Tony, and Jeff. On the surface, they looked like three ordinary, perfectly nice guys. They strutted out onto stage with more confidence than the first two, but then, again, that could hardly be considered a difficult feat. They calmly plugged in their electric guitars, and Tony sat down behind the drum set that had been placed on the stage. The surprise came when they started in on their song.

It was some sort of avant garde creation, I suppose. To the rest of us, it sounded like noise. The whole thing consisted of loud, discordant chords and Todd and Jeff calling out the names of colors at the tops of their lungs: "Red! Yellow! Pink! Puce!"

"Puce?" Saul and I repeated simultaneously. Al shushed us, but only someone who was bionic could have heard us over the noise of the electric guitars.

The song seemed to go on forever. Even Rusty O'Shea began to look distressed. When it was finally over, there was a burst of cheering from the back of the auditorium. All female voices. The three of them had apparently managed to build up quite a following.

"Thank you, boys," Rusty said diplomatically once he was back onstage again. "Our third contestant is Lisa Evans. Lisa is a junior. . . ."

"Hey, where *is* she?" I asked, looking around. "I *know* her, and she's not here. Where did she go?"

Al was preoccupied with the same question. He raced around the band room, throwing open the doors of the tiny practice rooms, searching the storerooms that housed the tubas and the music stands. He even took a quick run through the halls surrounding the auditorium. No Lisa.

"I guess she just couldn't take the pressure of show biz," someone in line behind me commented. "Too bad. I heard her doing her song, and it was really nice."

After Al had communicated the state of things to Rusty O'Shea via hand signals from the wings, he came running over to us.

"Okay, guys. That means you two are on next."

"Us?" I croaked.

He glanced at his clipboard and frowned. "You're Sallie and Saul, right?"

"Yeah, that's us," Saul answered for me. "Go ahead and announce us. We're ready."

Al gave Rusty the high sign, and I became totally numb. All I remember is Saul bodily pushing me onstage. He had a big smile on his face, and I tried to copy his every move. At first all I could see was lights. But then my eyes adjusted to the glare, and I began to see faces. None that I could recognize, just blurry little collections of eyes and noses. I stood frozen in front of the microphone. My mind went blank.

"Good evening, ladies and gentlemen." When I heard the unexpected sound of Saul's voice, I suddenly snapped back into the reality of what was happening. I glanced over at him, and saw that he was standing calmly in front of his microphone, beaming at the crowd, looking as relaxed as if he were standing in my living room.

"My name is Saul, and this is my partner, Sallie. Actually, I'm taking too much credit. Sallie here is really the brains of this outfit. I'm really *her* partner."

The crowd was warming up to him; I could feel it. I was amazed. No one else had said a word to the audience, except for Rusty O'Shea, of course. And here Saul was acting as if he had the world on a string.

"Tonight we'd like to do a song we wrote together. It was inspired by a very special lady, who is a friend of mine and a friend of Sallie's. I'm pretty sure she's out in the audience tonight, and if she is, I'd like to dedicate this song to her."

He strummed the opening chords of "If That Someone Else Is You," and I automatically joined in. We had run through that song so many times that it was second nature by then. I think my voice sounded a little shaky at first, but it wasn't long before I got caught up in singing. Before we had finished the first stanza, I realized that I was having the time of my life.

"Or if when she looks into my eyes, she doesn't quite see me," I sang, my voice sounding clearer and surer than ever before. It was a pretty song, and I could feel the audience responding to it. It was magic, what was happening out there. Never before had I experienced anything quite like it.

When we finished, there was a split second of total silence. I held my breath, not knowing what to expect. But what followed was thunderous applause and cheering. Cheering! And the voices that were raised in admiration were not even those of Rachel or Jenny or anybody else that I recognized. It was all sincere!

I could have stood on that stage bowing and smiling from ear to ear all night. But Saul had to drag me off, just as he had had to drag me on.

"See?" he teased once we were offstage. "I told you I'd have to pull you off that stage!"

"I want to sing more!" I cried. "Don't make me go backstage!"

"Just listen to that applause!" Saul insisted. "I think we've already managed to please that crowd. Even Rusty can't get a word in."

It was true. We brought down the house. The next contestant, a sophomore named Ralph, looked at us mournfully as he waited for the applause to subside so he could go on.

"You guys sure are a hard act to follow!" he exclaimed. Saul just smiled, but I chortled gleefully.

"They loved it! They loved it!" I kept saying over and over again. "Oh, Saul, do you think we'll win?"

"Let's go outside, Sallie. I think we could both use some air."

Once we were safely outside, behind the school, Saul leaned against the wall and grinned at me. "Well, they loved us in New York!" he cried, and we hugged each other and jumped up and down and squealed, all at once.

"Hey, you guys want to keep it down?" an annoyed voice called to us. "We don't want the audience to hear all this commotion."

I looked around and saw a boy about our age standing in the doorway. "Sorry," I said. "We didn't think anybody would be able to hear us from out here."

"That's okay. Just cool it, all right?" He walked over and peered at us in the dim light from a distant streetlight. "Hey, you two are the ones who just went on, aren't you? Your song was terrific! I really liked it. Especially that part at the end of each stanza, where you would pause, and then go on, 'Then it's okay.'"

"I thought of putting that pause in," I said proudly. "I'm glad you liked it. Are you entering the contest? Because if you are, you'd better go inside before Al discovers that you're missing."

He just laughed. "No. I work for the radio station. I do all the dirty work. Moving the equipment, things like that. My name is Nick."

"Hi, Nick. I'm Sallie, and this is Saul."

"I know. I saw your entire performance, and it was great. Where'd you guys learn to play guitar like that?"

"Oh, just from fooling around with it." I blushed. "It's really quite simple."

"Really? I'd love to learn."

"Maybe Sallie will give you a few lessons," Saul suggested lightly.

"Saul!" I scolded him, hoping Nick couldn't hear me.

"So you work for the station," Saul went on. "That sounds interesting."

"Actually, I just work part-time. A couple of evenings a week. My father works there, and whenever they need someone to do odd jobs, they call me. It's kind of fun."

"And what do you do the rest of the time?" I asked.

"I'm a senior at the Bronx High School of Science."

"Excuse me," Saul interrupted, "if you don't mind, Sallie, I think I'm going to duck into the auditorium and see if I can find Rachel. I want to find out how she liked our performance."

"I'm sure she loved it," I called after him as he disappeared back into the school.

"Is this Rachel the one the song was dedicated to?" Nick asked.

"Yes. She's his girlfriend. Well, I guess she is. They really just started going out together."

"So tell me, Sallie Spooner. What do you do when you're not writing songs?"

Nick leaned against the doorway, and for the first time I was able to get a good look at him, thanks to the bright lights of the school hallway. He was extremely good-looking, with curly light brown hair and hazel eyes. He was tall, but he seemed at ease with himself, not like some guys my age who spring up four inches overnight and then spend the next three years knocking over lamps and walking into tables.

"Well, I'm a senior here. That takes up a lot of time. And I like to read, and go to the movies, and just hang around with Rachel . . . she's my best friend."

"So you don't think you could find any time to teach me a few chords on the guitar, huh?" Nick teased me.

In my usual fashion I responded by blushing. I hoped the dim light of the alleyway I was lurking in would hide my red cheeks from Nick.

"Well, I don't know. . . ."

"How about if we made a deal, then?"

"What kind of deal?"

"Let's see. You just told me you like to go to the movies. So how about this: I'll take you to the movie of your choice if you agree to teach me five of your favorite chords. And, hopefully, they'll be chords that can be put together to make a song."

I thought for a few seconds. For some unknown reason, I kept thinking that I could teach Nick "The Streets of Laredo" in less than half an hour. "Okay," I agreed. "That sounds fair."

"How about next weekend? Say, Friday night?"

"All right."

"Great! We've got a date, then. Here, let me write down your telephone number."

Fate is such a funny thing. If Saul and I hadn't gone out to get some air, I might never have met Nick. But there was no time for thinking about life's little surprises that night. Once things were all set with Nick, I excused myself and went back into the school to find Saul. After all, we'd have to be around for the moment of truth, when the winners were announced.

I crept back into the band room and managed to catch the last three or four songs. Not bad, I concluded after I heard each one, but hardly anything to worry about. I felt positively smug as I waited for all the other contestants to take their turns.

When the last person was done and everyone agreed that Lisa Evans was undoubtedly long gone, Rusty O'Shea took his place at the microphone for the last time.

"Okay, folks, that's it for the competing songs. But

before we announce the winners, let me take a moment to introduce the three judges.''

Saul and I listened carefully. We wanted to make sure we knew exactly who it was who was sitting out there in the front row, determining our fates. The judges included our school principal, an executive from WROX, and a representative from one of the major record companies.

"Gee," I said, "I'm glad they didn't introduce the judges until the end. I would have been having fits if I knew that guy from Ace Records was here!"

"No, you wouldn't have. You're a pro!"

"Judges, are you ready with your decision?" There was a dramatic pause as one of them handed an envelope to Rusty O'Shea. I grasped Saul's arm so tightly that I'm surprised they didn't have to amputate.

"Third prize, and the winner of ten record albums from Ace Records and two free tickets to the Billy Joel concert at Madison Square Garden . . . Charlie MacDougal and Ellen Rubin, for their song, 'One Spring Day.' Charlie and Ellen!"

They gasped, then hugged each other, then ran out onto the stage. They seemed as happy as if they had just won a summer house in the south of France.

"I think they're just glad they managed to get through it," Saul said.

"Second prize, and the winner of twenty record albums from Ace and four tickets to the Billy Joel concert . . . Sylvia Romanoff."

As Sylvia drifted onstage, smiling serenely, Saul and I watched in silence. Neither of us felt like making jokes or light conversation at that point. Saul grabbed my arm, and the two of us just stood there, clutching at each other for dear life.

"And now is the moment you've all been waiting for.

The winners of the first prize. First prize consists of fifty free record albums, six tickets for the concert, and the chance to compete in the citywide competition. The winner of that second level of the contest will have his or her song recorded by one of the top groups in the industry. So as you can see, this prize is the big one.

"And the winner is . . . oh, I'm sorry, the winners *are* . . . Sallie Spooner and Saul Rodriguez, 'If That Someone Else Is You'!"

I continued staring at Rusty's profile, unaware that I had begun making quiet whimpering sounds. I stood there, unmoving, until I heard Saul saying, "Sallie! We won! Come on, we've got to go onstage!"

I followed him, like a robot, back onto the stage, in front of the blinding lights. We had won! My dream was no longer just a dream; it was a reality!

"We won?" I said as Rusty O'Shea handed us an envelope. It was a pretty silly thing to say, but the applause was so loud that no one could hear me anyway. I saw the lights of flashbulbs, and I realized that my whole family must be standing a few feet away, applauding and yelling. And Rachel was probably there, and Jane, and Sharon . . . all my friends. I think it was that realization, even more than the fact that Saul and I had actually won, that made me start crying.

And then it was over. The curtains were drawn closed, and Rusty O'Shea went back to being a surly middle-aged man. The other contestants offered their congratulations, some sincere, some halfhearted, then drifted away. I was in a daze as Saul and I put on our coats and bundled up our guitars.

When we stepped out into the hall, a small crowd was waiting for us: my family, Rachel, most of my other friends. They were all exuberant, and I felt like a real celebrity as they swarmed around me and Saul and hugged us. If I hadn't felt as if I were in another world, it probably would have been the happiest night of my life.

"How do you feel?" Jenny asked when things had calmed down a bit.

"Wonderful. Do you really have to ask?"

"Are you still up for coming over?" Rachel asked.

"Saul?" I asked. "Are you?"

He nodded. "Me, too. Let's go."

I said good-night to my parents, then Saul and Rachel and I linked arms and set off for the Glasses' apartment. The dazed feeling was starting to fade, and a sense of euphoria had begun to replace it.

"You know, guys," I said as we started across the street, "I hope I can remember this moment for the rest of my life. Because I want you both to know that at this very second, I am one happy lady!" I squeezed my two friends, and we continued on our way.

12

We didn't have to tell Dr. and Mrs. Glass who had won the WROX contest. Our whoops and screeches and uncontrollable giggles as the three of us burst through the front door of Rachel's apartment made an official announcement unnecessary. The Glasses were both seated calmly on the living room couch, absorbed in some old Katharine Hepburn movie that was on television. They glanced up, looking as if their home had just been invaded by Martians, then immediately deduced from our wild, intoxicated mood that our team had scored the victory of the evening.

"Don't tell me!" Mrs. Glass exclaimed, rising from the couch and taking off the glasses she always wore when watching TV. "Sallie Spooner walked off with first prize!"

"That's right," I squealed. "Saul and I are the grand champions!"

After a few more minutes of hugging and animallike noises and jumping up and down, not to mention a lot of excited questions and congratulations from Rachel's parents, Dr. Glass extended his hand toward Saul and said, "I don't believe we've had the pleasure of meeting. I'm Mitchell Glass, Rachel's father."

"I'm pleased to meet you. I'm Saul."

"Rachel told us you had entered the songwriting contest, Sallie," Mrs. Glass said, "but I hadn't realized you had a partner."

"Really? Maybe it's because Saul and I have only been partners for a couple of weeks."

"Well, it's apparently an association that has paid off." She smiled. "Congratulations to both of you. I'm so thrilled!"

"Yes, that is wonderful news," Dr. Glass agreed. "We'll have to make sure we're there at the finals."

"You bet," Rachel said. Then, turning to Saul and me, she moaned, "I don't know about you guys, but I am completely drained after that ordeal. I've been nervous for you both all night! I need a root beer in the worst way."

"*You!*" I cried. "What about *us*? We're the ones who were suffering onstage. Not to mention the torture of waiting it out in the wings!"

"I would have died if that had been me up there. Weren't you nervous, Sallie?"

"Not at all," Saul answered for me, despite the fact that my mouth dropped open and I stared at him aghast. "Our Sallie here was as relaxed as Johnny Carson himself."

"I was?" I croaked.

"Sure. Now, how about those root beers? Singing can be tough on the throat."

The three of us adjourned to the kitchen, where Rachel poured us mugs of cold soda with lots of ice. I started to gulp mine down, but then Rachel said, "Hey, how about a toast?"

"Okay," I agreed. "What shall we toast?"

"To your success!"

"To our success!"

We demolished our root beers, and then Rachel said, "Okay. Now, you guys have to go into the living room for a while. There's something I have to do in here."

"Oh, boy! A surprise!" I glanced over at Saul, but he didn't notice. He was too busy looking at Rachel with glowing eyes. "We do as we're told. Come on, Saul, let's go talk to Rachel's parents."

She gave him a peck on the cheek, then pushed us both out the door.

"You've never met Rachel's parents before, have you?" I whispered.

"Nope, this is the first time. They seem like nice people."

"They're great." Then I called jovially, "Excuse us, but we've just been banished from the kitchen. Is it all right if we join you?"

"Please do. The movie just ended, in fact." Mrs. Glass glanced up at us, and there were tears in her eyes. "Don't mind me," she explained. "Old Katharine Hepburn movies always make me cry. Have a seat, and tell me all about the competition."

"Let's see," I started babbling, "there were supposed to be fifteen entries, but one of them, a junior girl I know, just disappeared and never went on. I guess she got too nervous at the last minute.

"There were all kinds of entries. There was this punk rock-type song, where the lyrics consisted of the names of colors, and there were a whole bunch of folk songs—"

"Well, when do we get to hear this prize-winning musical composition?" Dr. Glass interrupted. "Or do we have to wait and buy the record?"

"Oh, yes, sing it for us!" Mrs. Glass exclaimed.

At that point Rachel's voice called from the kitchen, "Not yet! Not yet! Everybody stay where you are! Mom, turn out the lights, please."

She appeared in the doorway, balancing a huge white frosted cake, all aglow with candles, on a tray. When she drew nearer, we gathered around and read what she had just written on top with pale blue icing: CONGRATULATIONS, SALLIE AND SAUL.

"Those little blue blops around the edges are supposed to be notes," she explained apologetically.

"It's beautiful! Even the notes. But what would you have written if Saul and I had *lost*?"

"That's a good question." Rachel laughed. "I suppose, 'Better luck next time!'"

"That was a lovely idea, Rachel," her mother said. "Mitch, I'll make some coffee. It looks as if a little party has just materialized right here in our living room."

"So, tell me, Saul," Dr. Glass said when the five of us had sat down at the round dining room table. "Do you go to school with Sallie and Rachel? I'm surprised we've never met before."

"No. Actually, I live in Brooklyn. I only met Sallie a few weeks ago. We ran into each other at a party, and we formed a partnership so we could enter the WROX contest together." He looked over at me and grinned. "And then I met your daughter through Sallie."

"I guess any friend of Sallie's automatically becomes a friend of Rachel's, and vice versa." Mrs. Glass laughed. "I think it's terrific that you two are such close friends, and that you both see eye-to-eye on everything."

Rachel and I just smiled at each other a bit sheepishly.

"That's true," I said. "I don't know what Rachel and I would do if we didn't have each other."

"You know," Dr. Glass interjected suddenly, a twinkle in his eye, "I'd say that this calls for a toast. But I'm afraid that since we have no champagne, I'll have to raise my coffee cup to you." He stood up and said in a dramatic voice, "And so I propose a toast to three of the most charming people I have ever known. To Miss Spooner, of course, a longtime friend." He bowed toward me. "To Miss Glass, my favorite daughter. And to Mr. . . . hmm, I'm afraid I never did catch your last name, Saul."

"Rodriguez," he answered.

Now, I couldn't swear that I saw two raised eyebrows, one in one corner of the room, one exactly opposite it, but I did sense just a tad of tension all of a sudden. Still, after one or two quick glances were exchanged, the lively mood picked up where it had left off.

"To Mr. Rodriguez," Dr. Glass continued, "the Glass family's newest friend."

After we had drunk a sip of whatever beverage each of us was having, and Rachel's cake had been cut into such generous portions that I feared for the future of my waistline, our lighthearted banter drifted on to other assorted topics.

But as the last crumbs were being scraped off our plates and seconds had been reluctantly refused, there was a lull in the conversation. Mrs. Glass said offhandedly, "Tell me, Saul, is your last name a Spanish name?"

"Yes, it is. I'm Puerto Rican."

"How unusual. With your first name being Saul . . ."

The same dialogue that Saul and I had run through the first night I met him was rerun between him and Mrs. Glass. The Sol-versus-Saúl-pronunciation-of-his-name business. It was obvious that Mrs. Glass's thought process had been identical to mine. Between Saul's first name and his physical appearance, she had naturally assumed he was Jewish. And so it was a surprise—if not a shock—to discover otherwise. But that surprise was only momentary. After a brief discussion about the pronunciation of his name, the Glasses sat back as Saul and I prepared to serenade them.

It was with great pride that we launched into "If That

Someone Else Is You." After all, not only was it quickly becoming our favorite song, it was now wearing a blue ribbon from WROX. And that was no small honor. In loud, gusty voices, we sang:

> If someone leaves me waiting on the corner for an hour,
> Or forgets she left the milk out of the fridge and it turns
>   sour,
> Or forgets that it's my birthday or forgets to leave the
>   key,
> Or argues with the traffic cop when I'd rather let it be,
>
> Then I start to feel
> Maybe I was wrong;
> That I'm spending too much time with her
> And not enough with my simple songs.
>
> Then I say
> Maybe it should end.
> But if that someone else is you—
> Then it's okay.

Dr. and Mrs. Glass listened with little smiles on their faces, and they even bopped along a bit to the tune. Rachel just beamed proudly. Everything seemed to be moving along smoothly until we started on the third verse:

> If someone says she's crystal and that I am only glass,
> That our two worlds are different and our love could
>   never last,
> "But both of them are fragile, they need tender care," I
>   claim,
> "And if both of them shatter, then they both would look
>   the same,"
>
> Then I start to feel
> Maybe I was wrong;
> That I'm spending too much time with her
> And not enough with my simple songs.
>
> Then I say
> Maybe it should end.
> But if that someone else is you—
> Then it's okay.

Maybe it was because the faintest hint of a blush colored Rachel's cheeks, maybe it was because Saul was looking directly at her as he sang the words. At any rate that barely perceptible level of tension that I had picked up on earlier when Saul had mentioned his last name returned. Only this time it seemed a whole lot stronger. I was certain that I saw Dr. and Mrs. Glass exchange meaningful, as well as puzzled, glances.

But we finished up our brief performance without mishap. All three members of the audience applauded enthusiastically; then Saul and I were both duly modest.

"What a lovely song!" Mrs. Glass exclaimed.

"It is a catchy melody." Dr. Glass nodded. "I'll be carrying that around in my head for days. I'll be tapping my toe as I write out prescriptions. I'll become known as the Singing Dermatologist."

"I hate to be a party pooper"—Mrs. Glass sighed, looking at her watch—"but it is getting late. Between the excitement of this musical victory and that heart-wrenching Katharine Hepburn movie, I'm about worn out. If you don't mind, I'm going to bed." She kissed me and Rachel, then shook Saul's hand. "Thank you for a wonderful evening, and congratulations, again, to both of you. Rachel, don't stay up too late."

"I'll be moving on, too," Dr. Glass said. "Good night."

"I'll clean everything up," Rachel assured them. "Good night."

The Glasses wandered off to their bedroom, and the three of us who remained set about bringing cups and saucers into the kitchen and wrapping up the remains of Rachel's glorious cake.

"You two don't have to help," Rachel protested. "After all, you're stars!"

"Nonsense," I said. "Success hasn't spoiled us. We're

still the same charming, modest, wonderful people we always were. Right, Saul?"

"Right. In fact, we're even *more* charming and modest and wonderful now!"

"If you can come back to earth for a minute," Rachel teased, swatting at Saul with a dish towel, "how about if I wash, Saul dries, and Sallie brings in all the dishes from the dining room?"

We busied ourselves with our respective tasks. I was back in the dining room, piling cups and glasses and saucers onto a tray, hoping my occasional accident-proneness would not choose this particular moment to return, when Mrs. Glass reappeared.

"I forgot to remind Rachel to leave the top lock of the front door undone. Steve is coming in late tonight, and he only has a key for the bottom lock. Here, let me help you with those." She swooped up a pile of saucers and spoons, and the two of us carried our loads into the kitchen.

As Mrs. Glass pushed against the swinging door that separated the kitchen from the dining room, she let out a gasp. Through the doorway, over her shoulder, I could see what it was that was responsible for her unexpected reaction. Saul and Rachel were standing next to the refrigerator, locked in an embrace, kissing.

I don't know which was more difficult; keeping myself from dropping the stack of saucers I was carrying or keeping my big mouth shut. Fortunately, I was able to do both.

"Rachel!" Mrs. Glass cried, partly from shock, partly as a means of making her daughter aware that she was there.

Saul and Rachel pulled apart, then blinked at us with looks of surprise and guilt on their faces.

"Mom!" Rachel cried. "I thought you'd gone to bed."

It was an irrelevant remark, of course, but also the most obvious thing to say. Mrs. Glass and I had entered the kitchen by then, and I just stood there, wishing I could disappear. I thought morosely, Oh, that this too, too solid flesh would melt, as one of Shakespeare's characters once said. It is not often that I was poetic, but at that point I needed something to distance myself from the uncomfortable situation I had literally just walked into.

Never before had I seen Mrs. Glass so angry, and never before had I seen anger so well controlled. She remained poised, if tight-lipped, as she said, "Rachel, it's very late. Don't you think it would be best if Saul were to start home? He must have a long subway ride ahead of him."

Rachel and Saul glanced at each other, looking torn and reluctant, then Saul agreed. He was certainly not blind to what was going on. He, too, remained poised and controlled. He said good night to us, thanked Mrs. Glass for the evening, then exited out the swinging door. All three of us remained silent until we heard the front door of the apartment close.

"Well, Rachel," Mrs. Glass said in that same controlled tone. "I think you and I had better have a talk. I'll ask your father to walk Sallie home."

"That's not necessary," I protested. "It's only a few blocks."

"I'd like Sallie to stay," Rachel said evenly. "Whatever you have to say to me, Mom, I think it's important that Sallie hear it, too."

Mrs. Glass and I looked at each other, then she gestured for Rachel and me to sit down at the kitchen table with her. I waited expectantly, not sure if I should be curious about what was going to follow or filled with dread. At any rate I resolved not to say a single word.

"Well, Rachel," Mrs. Glass began, "do you want to begin, or shall I?"

"I know what you're going to say," Rachel replied. "You're upset because I'm going out with Saul Rodriguez. Not only is he not Jewish, he's Puerto Rican."

"Let's take this one step at a time. First of all, I didn't know you were going out with *any* boy. How long has this been going on?"

"There really isn't anything 'going on.' Saul and I went out to the movies one night, and it happened to be a night when you and Daddy weren't around. I think you had gone out to dinner."

"I don't mind your going out when we're not home, Rachel, but why didn't you at least tell me?"

"I don't know." Rachel shrugged. "I guess I figured it wasn't that important. All we did was go to a movie on Eighty-sixth Street. If it had been Sallie I was going with, I wouldn't have bothered to mention it, either."

"It's not quite the same thing. Rachel, it's only for your safety that your father and I like to know who you're going out with. In the future please let me know. Not so I can approve or disapprove, but so I know what you're doing and where you're going and who you're going with. Okay?"

"Okay, that's fair," Rachel agreed. "Now, speaking of approving and disapproving—"

"Rachel, Saul seems like a lovely fellow. And he was a friend of Sallie's even before you met him, right?" I nodded. "That's a good enough recommendation right there, as far as I'm concerned. But naturally I have some concerns over the fact that he isn't Jewish. Maybe 'concerns' isn't the right word. Perhaps 'questions' is."

"Not to mention the fact that Saul is Puerto Rican," Rachel said defensively. I had to stare at her to assure myself that it really was Rachel Glass who was uttering these words. I had to admit, for all the tension in the room, this was proving to be an enthralling discussion.

"You've always gone out with Jewish boys in the past. Why is this time different?"

"Maybe it's because Saul is different," Rachel said quickly. Then, more calmly, she went on, "To tell you the truth, when I first met Saul, I assumed he was Jewish, just as you probably did. Saul is generally a Jewish name, and he does look Jewish." She cast a hasty glance in my direction, one that seemed vaguely apologetic. "Anyway, it wasn't until I had spent the entire evening with him and really started to like him that I found out he was Puerto Rican. And then I was extremely torn. Sallie can attest to that.

"Oh, Mom, I've given this a lot of thought. I know everything you're thinking. You've taught me the importance of the Jewish tradition, and I have a strong sense of what that means. And it's true that I've always gone out with boys who were Jewish. I know how unusual this situation is.

"I also know that the fact that Saul is Puerto Rican complicates things even further. Everyone knows how Puerto Ricans are viewed, especially in New York. And I can't deny that I thought about that, too, at first.

"But now that I know Saul, he's not Catholic or Puerto Rican. All he is is him, Saul. And since that's all I can see, that's all that's important to me." She paused and stared at the table for a few seconds. "I'm only seventeen, Mom. I know I'm not a child anymore, but I'm not an adult yet, either. I'm still trying to grow and to learn. I'm not getting ready to marry Saul; I just like being with him. And . . . and I'd like to continue seeing him." She looked up at her mother. "Unless you forbid me to, of course."

"No, I wouldn't do that, Rachel. You're right; you're not a child anymore, and I don't intend to treat you like one. You're old enough to decide who you want to see and who you don't want to see. I must say, however, that I am disappointed. I thought you had stronger ties to your religion, to the whole Jewish heritage. I realize that you're not about to marry Saul, but I thought you would be more interested in cultivating relationships with Jewish boys.

And the fact that Saul is Puerto Rican . . . well, you couldn't have found someone with a background more different from yours if you had tried."

As I watched this scene, I remained silent, but my eyes were wide as they stayed focused on Rachel's face. I listened to Mrs. Glass's words, and they did not surprise me. After all, she was merely repeating what she had said to me the week before. But I kept waiting for Rachel to argue with her, or at least say *something*. She, too, remained silent.

"Well, that's really all I have to say. It's late, and I think we should both get to bed. I'm sure Sallie's parents don't want her out at this hour." Mrs. Glass stood up and slowly pushed her chair to the kitchen table. "I'm not asking you to make a decision now. But I trust you, Rachel, and I know that you'll come to the one that's right for you. Good night."

For a long time, neither Rachel nor I said anything. We just sat at the table, listening to the silence of the apartment, each of us lost in her own thoughts. Finally, when I could stand it no more, I ventured, "I guess I'd better get going."

I waited for her to protest, but she merely looked at me with sad, confused eyes. I started for the door, then hesitated. "So what happens now?" I asked.

Rachel gave me a long, soulful look, then blinked her eyes hard. "Funny, I was just going to ask you the exact same thing, Sallie," she answered in a voice so soft that I could barely hear her.

13

Never let it be said that Sallie Spooner is not one heck of a resourceful person. Besides walking, eating, and looking at dinosaur bones, I have a score of other possible ways of dealing with my problems and tensions. In fact, I had never even realized how good I was at distracting myself until that week following the Saturday night of the WROX contest and the ensuing discussion on Rachel's social life.

I didn't see very much of her during that time. Oh, we passed each other in the hall at school, and we continued making our nightly phone calls to each other, but things were not the same. We were distant, Rachel and I, and it was because she was so torn up about this conflict with Saul. It was the first time she had ever had a major disagreement with her family, and it was the first time she had had to sit down and decide exactly where her priorities lay. It was a tough time for her, and as close as we were, I could do little to make things easier. So I just made sure she knew I was around and busied myself with other things.

There were plenty of old standbys to occupy my time. I think I saw about four thousand movies—some with other

141

friends, some with Jenny, some by myself. I read a lot. I even wrote a nifty little duet for guitar and piano.

As much as I hate to admit it, I had sort of forgotten about Nick. That's not quite as terrible as it probably sounds. All I mean is, I became so wrapped up in everything else that was going on that it took me a few seconds to remember who he was that Tuesday night when he called me up.

"Sallie, telephone!" Jenny came bounding into my room after dinner, pulling me out of the world of Chicago in the 1890s as I plowed through Dreiser's *Sister Carrie*. "It's a boy," she went on, so loudly I was convinced that whoever was on the other end of the wire must be blushing down to his sneakers. Then I realized that it was probably Saul, and I dragged myself to the phone.

I didn't particularly feel like talking to Saul, because I had no idea what I could say, so there was noticeable reluctance in my voice as I said hello.

"Hello, Sallie?"

"Yes, this is Sallie." It wasn't Saul's voice, but I couldn't imagine whose it was. "Who's this, please?"

"This is Nick. Remember? From the WROX contest? You know, the guy with all the electrical wires wrapped around his neck."

"Oh, yes, of course." I laughed. "I'm sorry, Nick. It's just that I've been in another world these days. How are you?"

"I'm fine. How about you? Has the excitement of winning the songwriting contest worn off yet?"

"My feet are back on the ground again, that's for sure. School and tests and parents have a way of bringing things right back into perspective. I'm still really pleased about it, though."

"You should be. You and that guy were terrific!"

"Thanks, but we still have the second level of the contest

in two weeks. That'll be the tough part. This first level was kid stuff."

"You'll be great. Besides, don't forget that I'll be there, rooting for you from backstage."

"Oh, will you? I didn't realize that you'd be working that night." I was genuinely glad, and I could feel the familiar rush of pinkness to my cheeks. Fortunately Jenny was off in her room somewhere. I was not in the mood for any more of her teasing, not after that whole fiasco with Saul.

"Are you busy practicing every minute of the day," Nick went on, "or will you still be able to find a few hours to teach this humble soul the joys of musical expression?"

"I think I could manage an hour or two," I joked.

"Great. So, then we're still on for Friday night? How about if we start with a movie, just as I promised, and then you can teach me a few chords?"

"Sounds fair."

"I have a slight problem, though," he said. "I don't have a guitar."

"That's okay. We can use mine until you decide if you're musically inclined or not."

"I suspect that I'm not. Unfortunately, science and the arts don't usually mix too well."

"That's not true!" I protested. "Look at Dr. Albert Schweitzer! When he was in Africa curing the natives, he used to spend every evening playing the organ!"

"Really? I didn't know that. Well, maybe there is hope for me, after all."

We agreed on the time he would come pick me up, and I told him my address. By the time I hung up the phone, I felt so lighthearted that a huge smile had begun to occupy my face full-time. I was happier than ever that Jenny wasn't around.

With Friday night's date a definite thing, my mood improved considerably. I began to feel that I was spending too much time thinking about other people and not enough thinking about myself. Still, some things are easier said than done, and I continued to worry about both Rachel and Saul, separately as well as together.

Then, something finally gave way on Thursday night. Jenny and I had just come home from seeing a French movie over on Second Avenue. It had been fun, and we had topped off the evening by stopping off for hot-fudge sundaes at Swensen's, an ice cream parlor right across the street from the theater. All the way home, she and I kept up a hilarious dialogue, using these ridiculous French accents. We both laughed hysterically for ages, and I ended up with a stomachache.

Anyway, we had just come home, and I was standing in front of my closet trying to decide what I would wear the next evening on my date with Nick. I'm always very particular about things like that when I'm going on a first date with someone. I heard the doorbell ring, which was kind of strange, because it was so late. Not just anyone can float by our doorman without being announced, so I knew it had to be someone near and dear to the Spooner family who had made his or her way to our humble abode at that unusual hour. When there was a cautious knock at the door of my bedroom, I knew it had to be Rachel.

"Come on in, Rachel," I called.

Sure enough, it was she. She opened the door and stuck her head in.

"Hi, Sallie. Is it okay if I come in?"

"Sure. I was just trying to decide what to wear . . . oh, never mind. Have a seat."

We sat down on the floor together like two Indians, me in my turquoise chenille bathrobe (the one that always makes me—old carrot-top herself—look like a walking Howard Johnson's), Rachel in her jeans and a ski jacket. She was all out of breath, and her cheeks and eyes glowed. I could smell the cold night air on her.

"Sallie, I know it's late, but I had to talk to you. I'll get right to the point. I've been giving this whole thing a lot of thought . . . and I've decided not to see Saul anymore."

There it was. After all those minutes and hours and days spent agonizing over how this whole thing was going to turn out, there it was. Rachel had reached her decision.

I didn't know what to say. I was disappointed, of course, and Rachel knew it. After all, we had already been through all this once before. So I simply nodded and said, "Okay."

She looked at me sadly, and I could see the difficulty she had been having—and still was having—with this.

"You don't understand, do you." It was a statement, not a question.

"No. You know I don't. I never have understood."

"Even after what my mother said the other night? . . ."

I shook my head. "I understood what she said, and I know your line of thinking. But after knowing Saul as well as I do, and *liking* him as much as I do—as much as we *both* do . . ."

Rachel started to stand up. "I hoped you'd be on my side, Sallie. You know this hasn't been easy for me. But I have to do it this way."

"Have you told Saul yet?"

"Yes. As a matter of fact, I'm surprised he didn't tell you before I did."

"Was he very upset?" I asked softly.

"Yes, I'm afraid so."

I sighed, feeling sorrier for Saul than I did for Rachel. After all, he was the one who was being rejected, and on grounds that were entirely out of his control. And, as far as I was still concerned, completely irrelevant.

"Well, I guess that's it, then. Will you still be coming to hear us sing at the WROX contest next weekend?"

"I—I think it would be better if Saul and I just avoided

each other completely. You're not mad, are you?" she added quickly.

"Well, of course I'd like you to be there, but I suppose that, under the circumstances, there's really nothing I can do."

"Oh, Sallie, please don't hate me!" Rachel wailed.

"I don't hate you, Rachel. I guess I just need some time to get used to this. I thought everything had been settled, and you and Saul seemed really happy together. And now, all of a sudden, it's off again. It's not that easy to digest."

"I don't want to lose you as a friend! You have to accept my decision on faith. Please?"

"I'll try." I stood up, too, and we hugged each other. But even though we were pretending that things were back to normal, they weren't, really. Just as Rachel was confused about where her loyalties should lie, so was I. I needed time to think, to sort everything out.

"I should be getting home now," Rachel said distractedly.

"Okay. Good night, Rachel. I'll see you in school."

"Yeah. See you." And she was gone.

I didn't sleep very well that night. It was more because I couldn't decide what to think than because I was angry or disappointed. Rachel was my best friend, and so I should have been prepared to support her in anything, no questions asked. Wasn't that what friendship was all about? But maybe there came a time to draw the line, to say you couldn't agree with something because it was wrong, because it was hurting someone. This was even hurting Rachel, as far as I was concerned. I finally drifted off to sleep sometime after three A.M., still not having decided exactly what role I should be playing.

In school the next day Rachel and I made a point of avoiding each other. I felt terrible doing that, but with things so unresolved, I didn't know what else to do.

Fortunately a surprise quiz in music theory kept me distracted enough to get me through the day.

It was with a heavy heart that I dressed for my date with Nick. At that point I couldn't get very excited over the issue of purple sweaters versus striped blouses, and I ended up throwing on the most convenient outfit I could find. What difference does it make what you're wearing when your whole world is in turmoil? As I was brushing my hair halfheartedly, glowering at my reflection in the mirror and wondering about the meaning of life, I heard the doorbell ring.

He's early, I thought, glancing at my watch. Then Jenny's voice came through my closed bedroom door: "Sallie, it's Saul."

Saul! What was he doing here?

A dumb question, I reminded myself. He was looking for a friendly face, of course, perhaps even a sympathetic shoulder to cry on. But Nick was due in a few minutes. Oh, dear, I thought, what was the ethical thing to do? I didn't want to ruin my date, but Saul obviously needed me for moral support. I rushed into the living room, uncertain of what I would do.

"Hi, Sallie." Saul greeted me without much enthusiasm. "I guess you heard the latest news."

"Yeah, I heard. And I'm terribly sorry." We sat down on the couch together. I cast a dirty look at Jenny, and she disappeared without any hesitation. I thought to myself, Sometimes it seems that my little sister is actually growing up.

"Well, I don't want to bore you with all the gory details. And it really isn't your problem. I just thought maybe you and I could take in a movie, or go have a pizza. . . ."

"Oh, Saul, I'm sorry. I have a date with Nick tonight. Remember? The guy you and I met at the WROX competition?"

"Oh, that's right. I forgot about him." Saul looked so sad at that point that for a split second, I was willing to cancel my date entirely, or bring him along. I couldn't just abandon him, not when he looked so desperate.

But then a funny thing happened. Jenny walked into the room, looking as if she were about to start crying.

"Jenny! What happened?" I asked.

"It's my cassette player. I think it just died. And I've invited a bunch of kids over tomorrow to listen to some of my brand-new tapes. I just bought them!"

"Maybe you could get it fixed first thing tomorrow morning," I suggested, feeling completely helpless. "Or you could always borrow my record player. . . ."

"It's not the same thing," she insisted. "You can't play tapes on a record player."

"Maybe I could take a look at it," Saul suggested. "I'm pretty good at fixing things."

"Oh, Saul, *would* you? I'd appreciate it so much!" Jenny's face lit up like the Christmas tree at Rockefeller Center. She grabbed his arm and led him away. "It's right in my bedroom, on the desk. Oh, I'll be there in a second. Let me just tell Sallie something first. . . ."

She came running back to me and whispered, "Sallie, is that okay, what I just did?"

"What do you mean?" I looked at her, genuinely puzzled.

"Well, Saul sounded as if he was in pretty bad shape. . . ."

"You were eavesdropping!"

"Of course." She scowled. "Remember, you're talking to an honor student at the Little Sister Academy. Anyway, it seemed to me that Saul needed to be needed tonight."

"I'm still not sure I understand."

Jenny proudly held up a tiny screw and a little piece of wire.

"You lied!" I gasped.

"I didn't lie," she answered matter-of-factly. "My cassette player really *is* broken. At least, now it is. The only part I lied about is that business about my friends coming over tomorrow. I haven't bought a new tape since last August, either."

"You little devil!" I started laughing. Then I gave her a hug.

"What's that for?"

"For being so perceptive about people. And so sensitive to their needs. Now, you'd better scoot. Saul is going to need a screwdriver, if you want him to fix that thing!"

A few minutes later, when Saul was up to his elbows in wires and screws and Jenny was enjoying her role as a helpless *femme fatale*, Nick showed up, and we quickly ducked out.

"You certainly look pretty this evening," he commented as we started toward movie theater row, up on Eighty-sixth Street.

I glanced at him, surprised, then said thank-you. I could see already that he was a far cry from Dan Meyer and that whole breed known as "average teenage boys." Perhaps his maturity had something to do with his interest in science or the fact that he worked part-time. At any rate, I liked it.

"This has been quite an evening." I sighed, glad to be out with Nick, relaxing and just having a good time. "Actually, this has been quite a week."

"Don't tell me. It has to be either too much schoolwork, hassles from your parents, or"—his eyes twinkled in the neon lights of Eighty-sixth Street—"perhaps an argument with one of your boyfriends?"

"If you're trying to find out about my social life," I teased, "let me tell you that I'm not about to divulge any secrets. I intend to keep an air of mystery about me for as long as I can."

"With those freckles?" he returned. "Hah! I bet that all I'd have to do would be tickle you to get you to tell me anything I want to know. You look as if you're too impish to keep any secrets."

"Actually, you wouldn't even have to tickle me," I admitted. "Usually all people have to do is ask me something, and I end up talking their ears off for hours."

"Okay, then. What is it that's been troubling you this week?"

I found it very easy to talk to Nick. Maybe it was because he was such a good listener. I really hadn't intended to tell him the whole Rachel-and-Saul story, but somehow it all came pouring out. He listened sympathetically.

"Hmm," he said when I had finished, bringing him up to that same evening, when Saul had appeared on my doorstep for solace and companionship.

"It sounds to me as if there really is nothing you can do about this. And, after all, it does have nothing to do with you."

"I know. But Rachel is my best friend! And Saul is probably my *second* best friend. And they're perfect for each other. Even *they* know it. Just because she happens to be Jewish, and he happens to be Puerto Rican . . ."

"Look," Nick said calmly, taking my hand, "I think it's great that you're so concerned about your friends. It shows that you care about them a lot. But you just have to accept the fact that things have a way of working themselves out, and more often than not, they work out for the best. Now why don't you start worrying about more relevant issues?"

"Like?"

"Like whether a redheaded girl from Manhattan who writes songs can find true love and happiness with a brown-haired boy from Staten Island whose idea of a good time is spending hours in a lab with a Bunsen burner and a box full of test tubes."

"Oh, no!" I groaned. "Don't tell me you're a chemistry freak!"

"Is that bad? I know I told you I go to the Bronx High School of Science. . . ."

"No, it's not bad. It's just . . . ironic. Chemistry happens to be a particular nonfavorite of mine, that's all. It also happens to be where I first met . . . oh, never mind."

We were in the theater lobby by then, and as I glanced around at all the other couples, laughing and holding hands and buying popcorn, I realized that Nick was right. I was there to have a good time with him, and instead I was talking away a mile a minute about people that he didn't even know.

"I'll tell you what," I said flirtatiously. "I'll make a deal with you."

"Go on."

"I promise not to mention Saul or Rachel one more time this entire evening if you buy me some popcorn."

"Ho, ho, I see you can be bought. All right, it's a deal."

"After all, isn't that why you and I are going out tonight?"

"What do you mean?" Nick looked confused.

"Well, the night that you and I met, we made a deal. You said you'd take me to the movies if I taught you how to play the guitar. So isn't our entire relationship based on a deal we made?"

"Oh, yeah, that." He colored slightly. "I guess I have a confession to make."

"Yeah?"

"I happen to be tone-deaf."

We both laughed, and I kissed Nick on the cheek. This evening was turning out to be just what the doctor ordered.

14

The night before the finals for the WROX songwriting contest, when kids from all over the city would be competing for the grand prize of having their song recorded by one of the country's top rock groups, two major things happened. One of them was very good. I received one perfect red rose from a male admirer for the first time in my entire life—and the admirer was Nick. "Break a leg!" said the card. It was signed, "With love and devotion from your greatest fan." Now how could you not love the guy?

The second thing was not at all good. In fact, it was terrible. Saul called me up to tell me he had decided not to enter the competition after all.

"What do you *mean*?!" I screeched into the telephone, my voice reaching hysterical proportions. "We're a team! You can't let me down now!" Fantasies of such violent nature that I scared even myself began running through my mind.

"I know," he replied in a morose voice. "But I really don't feel much like singing. To tell you the truth, I don't feel like doing much of anything. I know that I wouldn't be able to do a good job, and we'd never win."

"Saul! Please! Don't do this to me!" I was near tears. "Can't you find someone else? How about Nick?"

"Nick happens to be completely tone-deaf."

"Maybe you could do it alone."

"The song is entered in both our names. Besides, the harmony is the best part. Please, Saul, I'll do anything. Anything at all!"

"Can you get Rachel to change her mind?"

I sighed, totally exasperated. Why me? I was thinking.

"Saul, listen to me. If you back out now, I'll die. I'll just die. You know how important this is to me. I'll never ask you for another favor for as long as I live. Ple-e-ase!"

There was a pause that seemed to last an eternity. I could feel the gray hairs sprouting all over my head.

"Well," he drawled, sounding so low that he could have been making the phone call from the bottom of a twenty-foot pit, "I guess I can do it."

"Oh, thank you, thank you!" My heart started beating again. "You'll be fine. You'll see. Once you're out there on the stage—the smell of the greasepaint, the roar of the crowd, or the roar of the greasepaint, the smell of the crowd . . ."

My attempt at levity went totally unnoticed and unappreciated.

"Yeah, well, I'll meet you there at eight, then."

"Seven-thirty, Saul. Seven-thirty. And do you have the address?"

"Yeah. I've got it written down somewhere. See you tomorrow then, Sallie." *Click.*

That was all I needed to transform my mood from mild butterflies in the stomach to hysterical bats throughout my entire body. During the next twenty-four hours, not only did I have to worry about the actual contest, I had to worry about whether the other half of the famed Spooner-and-Rodriguez team would even show up. Even the sight of that beautiful red rose smiling down at me from the dresser where it stood up straight in a cut glass vase could not turn me back into my usual happy-go-lucky self. What price fame? I found myself asking over and over again as I counted down the hours until the contest.

Still, things tend to be easier the second time around. Every action seemed familiar as I got ready that Saturday night, and there was great comfort in the realization that I had already managed to get myself through a similar ordeal once before. As I stood before my full-length mirror, examining myself one more time before heading out the front door, I said aloud, "You've done it before, Spooner, and you can do it again."

This time I insisted upon going it alone. Jenny would be coming later on with my parents. As I trekked over to the subway station, I discovered that a tremendous calm was falling over me. I really didn't know where all that sudden self-confidence was coming from, but I wasn't about to argue. I even started looking forward to the competition. I told myself that I was on my way to becoming a true pro.

The contest was being held in the huge auditorium of one of the high schools in mid-Manhattan. I didn't know exactly where it was, so I made sure I left myself plenty of time to get lost. As it turned out, however, I found the school with no trouble at all, and there were signs and arrows all over the place directing us strangers to the Choral Room. It was still so early that there were very few people around. There was one familiar face, however, and I snuck over and put my hands over the eyes of its owner.

"Guess who!" I cried, masking my voice. I sounded rather like a frog.

"Don't tell me. It's got to be The Spoon herself!" Nick whirled around and grinned at me.

"Oh, you're no fun. You guessed too easily."

"That's because your red hair was giving off sparks. I could see them between your fingers."

"Oh, you nut! By the way, thank you for the rose," I said, suddenly shy. "That was very sweet of you."

"Yeah, well, it was nothing." Nick turned beet-red. "So, anyway," he went on, obviously anxious to change the subject, "are you all set for tonight?'

"Oh, I hope so."

"What's the matter? You don't sound very certain."

"It's Saul. He called last night and said he wouldn't be able to make it tonight."

"What!"

"Don't worry, I changed his mind. At least, I think I did." My eyes remained glued to the door of the Choral Room, where other contestants had started trickling in. My heart jumped every time a male with dark hair or a guitar case or even a plaid flannel shirt walked in. None of them was Saul, however.

"He wouldn't back out on you at the last minute, would he?"

"Not voluntarily. But don't forget, a broken heart is a powerful thing. Oh, look!" I cried all of a sudden. "It's him! He's here!" I felt the way the French must have felt when the American soldiers landed at Normandy during World War II. "Saul! Saul! Over here!"

Once I saw that good old Saul had come through as promised, any traces of nervousness that had remained disappeared completely. The feeling of certain victory returned.

"Oh, hi, Sallie. Hello, Nick." Saul wandered over, his eyes vacant, his demeanor listless. I could tell his heart wasn't in this.

"Saul, aren't you excited?" I exclaimed, trying desperately to muster up some enthusiasm. "This is the night we've both been waiting for!"

"What? Oh, yeah." My plan didn't seem to be working.

"Well, I guess I'd better get back to work," Nick said. "I still have to check the mikes. Hey, good luck, you guys. I mean, break a leg. See you later." He gave me a brotherly pat on the back, then ran off to tend to his wires.

I decided to try a different tactic. "Saul," I said impatiently, "you'd better snap out of this. You promised you'd give it your best shot tonight." Actually, he'd promised nothing of the sort, but I was willing to resort to anything at that point. "As long as you've shown up, you could at least look a little less pained."

"I'm sorry, Sallie. I'll be okay once we get onstage. Here, I'll even tune my guitar." He took off his jacket and threw it over a chair, then started to unlock his guitar case. With every one of his deliberate movements I found myself growing more and more fidgety. It was as if at the first competition we had shared our nervousness, but this time I was doing the worrying for both of us.

Because Saul was too distraught to offer me any consolation or support, I decided to ignore him and instead concentrate on what was going on around me. And what a flurry of activity there was! As it grew closer to eight o'clock, the Choral Room became jam-packed with eager contestants, chattering away excitedly, with animated movements and bright, shining eyes. This group was much more diverse than the one that had gathered together in my high school band room two weeks earlier. There were some kids who looked really young, and some who looked so old I could hardly believe they were still in high school. There were black kids and Asian kids and preppie kids, and the instruments they were warming up on ranged from simple folk guitars to tambourines and xylophones to shrieking electric guitars with four-foot amplifiers.

And the clothes were so eclectic that I felt as if I were in the middle of a circus. I saw faded jeans and denim jackets, dark blue suits and ties, silver lamé hot pants and halters. New York City's high school kids were bursting with creativity and energy, and this was their chance to play it out to the fullest. I felt positively drab in my cautious little striped shirt and khaki pants. Still, I reminded myself, it was the music that counted tonight, not the musicians. And I remained confident that our offering was top-notch.

The room was sizzling with electricity as Al appeared, clapping his hands for attention. We all gathered around him, anxious for things to get started.

"Good evening, kids, and welcome to the finals for the WROX Songwriting Contest. First of all, I'd like to extend my congratulations to everyone in the room, since all of you are already winners. Everyone here has already won the first level of the competition at their respective high schools. Now, tonight we're going to be picking out the best songs from the entire city. We'll be awarding three prizes—first, second, and third—plus five honorable mentions. Good luck to each and every one of you.

"The format for tonight will be pretty much the same as the first level of the competition. I'll read through the list in the order you'll be appearing onstage, so please listen carefully. I'll be calling you by number, so remember the number that's been assigned to you."

He turned to the clipboard he had been holding at his side. "Okay. Number one is Wendy Greenberg and Jack Simmons. . . ."

There were forty entries in all. It was going to be a long night. Saul and I were Number eight.

"Is that good or bad, do you think?" I whispered when our names were read off the list.

"Pretty good, I'd say. Much better than being Number forty. I don't think anybody will be awake by then."

"Actually, I'm surprised there are only forty songs

entered in this thing. Considering how many high schools there must be in New York City . . ."

"Yes, but not every school had a competition, I'm sure. You might find this hard to believe, Sallie, but not everybody in the world dreams of becoming a songwriter."

"You're right," I agreed. "I do tend to forget that."

I was glad to see that Saul seemed to be returning to his normal self once again. By that point I just wanted to get the whole thing over with as quickly and as uneventfully as possible. I had gone beyond nervousness, beyond excitement . . . into the realm of the numb. Just let it be over soon, I pleaded silently.

The emcee for the evening was Rusty O'Shea again. Actually, I felt kind of sorry for him. I mean, what an awful way to spend your Saturday nights, hanging out at high schools all over the city, listening to pint-sized hopefuls sing their little hearts out. If I were Rusty O'Shea, a famous disc jockey, I decided, I'd much rather spend my Saturday nights running around town to chic clubs and fancy restaurants. Or at least staying home with a loved one, watching television and drinking beer. Anything other than standing on a stage, making cute comments about people who were complete strangers. But I guess entertainment is a funny business, and you just have to get used to it.

Because of the layout of the school auditorium, we were informed, the only way we could hear the other songs in the competition was through a loudspeaker that was hanging in one corner of the Choral Room. There would be no lurking in the wings this time around. So, I settled back into a wooden chair whose armrest was a little desk, prepared to listen to our first seven competitors.

"Good evening, ladies and gentlemen, and welcome to the finals of the WROX Songwriting Competition," came Rusty O'Shea's distinctive voice from out of nowhere. I must say, it really was like listening to the radio. I tried to relax, but I was tense as I waited to hear the other songs, waited to see how our song would measure up against New York's finest.

"Because we have a long program scheduled for this evening, let's get going right away. Our first song for tonight is by Wendy Greenberg and Jack Simmons of Grover Cleveland High. . . ."

While I had planned to hang on to every note that poured out of the loudspeaker, I found the next half hour blurring. To this day, I have no recollection of any of the music that I heard while I was waiting to go on. I guess I was really out of it, probably because I was even more nervous than I realized. Especially when I heard song Number seven being introduced.

"Well, Saul," I gulped, "I guess we're on next. This is it."

"Yup. Best of luck to you, buddy. I know we're going to knock 'em dead."

I felt as if I were in a dream as I followed Saul through the Choral Room, out to the hall. I clung to my guitar as if I were holding on for dear life. Foggy faces came and went, but none of them registered in my brain. I just went through the motions automatically, and the next thing I knew, Rusty O'Shea was announcing my name into the microphone.

I heard loud applause, I saw wires and bright lights as I shuffled across the stage, squinting and clearing my throat. Time and space ceased to exist; all there was was a vague awareness of Saul's presence next to me as we took our places in front of a microphone. And then, Saul's clear, confident voice cut through the din.

"Good evening, folks. My name is Saul, and this is my partner and friend, Sallie. The song we'd like to sing for you tonight is called 'If That Someone Else Is You,' and we hope you enjoy it as much as we're going to enjoy singing it for you." And he was off, strumming the familiar opening chords of our song.

Somehow, my mouth opened, the words came out, my fingers found the correct chords on my guitar. Without knowing how, I was singing our song.

> If someone leaves me waiting on the corner for an hour,
> Or forgets she left the milk out of the fridge and it turns
>   sour,
> Or forgets that it's my birthday or forgets to leave the
>   key,
> Or argues with the traffic cop when I'd rather let it be,
>
> Then I start to feel
> Maybe I was wrong;
> That I'm spending too much time with her
> And not enough with my simple songs.
>
> Then I say
> Maybe it should end.
> But if that someone else is you—
> Then it's okay.

As I was singing, it occurred to me that our song was very pretty, that it was clever, even. It was as if I were hearing it for the first time, probably because I felt so removed from the entire situation.

I like this song, I thought, as I raised my voice to blend my harmony in with Saul's husky rendition of the melody. It's a terrific song. And I started to smile as I went on singing.

Then it was over, and there was thunderous applause. Saul took my hand and we both bowed slightly, then exited offstage as calmly as we had walked on less than three minutes earlier.

"Is it over already?" I asked as I found myself back in the Choral Room.

"Yes, I'm afraid so. Or maybe I should say, 'Yes, thank heavens!'"

"How did we do?" Somehow, I felt as if I had missed the whole thing.

"We did great. Just great." Saul smiled at me and squeezed my hand. A wave of relief and tremendous fatigue swept over me, and my knees felt so weak that I returned to my creaky wooden chair.

The rest of the evening passed slowly. Song after song assaulted my ears, some fast and loud, some soft and bland, some with marked resemblances to other songs I knew well. They all blended together into one long mass of music, though, just as the first seven had. The only one that seemed at all memorable was ours. At least, as far as I was concerned.

Then, finally, I heard the invisible Rusty O'Shea announce heartily, "Well, ladies and gentlemen, that about wraps up our program for this evening. Let's have a round of applause for all the contestants, since they all did a tremendous job."

I glanced over at Saul, who was draped across the wooden chair next to mine. His face was drawn into a serious expression, and for the first time since we had started the whole process of planning and composing and competing, I realized that he wanted to win just as much as I did.

Rusty's voice broke through the rapidly dying out applause. "And now, judges, if you're ready with your decision . . ."

The judges had been introduced already, right before the fifteen-minute intermission. There were three of them: a WROX deejay, an executive from the station, and a woman who was a talent scout for a record company. Once again, when I found out the identity of those who were sitting in judgment of my musical talent, I was glad that while I was doing my stint, all they were to me were pale, distant faces in the crowd. Sometimes ignorance is the best policy.

The Choral Room was so quiet that you could have heard a guitar pick drop as we all listened to the barely perceptible crackling sound of an envelope being handed to Rusty O'Shea. Within that envelope, we all knew, lay our destinies. I looked around and saw a roomful of mannequins, frozen in place, ears cocked toward the loudspeaker.

"Okay," Rusty's voice boomed. "We'll start with our five honorable mentions. They're listed here in random order. Clyde Peters and Randy White!"

Each time a name was announced, one of the faces would break into some expression other than suspended animation. Some lit up into smiles; some tried to mask disappointment. And as each of the five spots was filled, the tension in the room increased even more. Saul and I clasped hands, clinging to each other like two Miss America finalists awaiting the name of the first runner-up.

When those five songs had been given their honorable mention and the composers had filed onto the stage to receive applause and some sort of prize in a plain unmarked envelope, it was time for the announcement of the winners of the third, the second, and the highly coveted first prize.

"And now, the winner of the third prize . . ."

"Come on, come on," I muttered as Rusty O'Shea went on endlessly about the twelve million record albums that went along with the distinction of walking off with third prize.

". . . Wendy Greenberg and Jack Simmons!"

Wendy and Jack shuffled out of the Choral Room in their matching black leather jeans, openly disappointed by having come so close to first prize, but having nothing to show for it except more records than Disco-Mat.

More applause, more tension. "Come on, come on." My patience was running out, and a mood closely approximating hysteria was moving in.

"The winner of second prize . . . Vincent Scala."

By that point Saul and I were as frozen as all the other mannequins in the room. I could hardly breathe.

"And now, here is the moment we've all been waiting for. As you know, the song that wins first prize in this year's WROX Songwriting Contest will be recorded by one of the top groups in today's recording industry. And that lucky person is . . ."

I inhaled sharply and dug my fingernails into my thighs.

"Or rather, the winners are . . ."

I closed my eyes tight and clenched my jaw.

"Elizabeth Humbard and Maria Diaz, for their song, 'I Loved You in the Morning.' Congratulations, Elizabeth and Maria!"

It took a few seconds for what had just happened to register. I continued sitting there—eyes closed, jaw clenched, breath held, fingernails clawing at my legs—even as the applause for Elizabeth and Maria died down. I heard people starting to move around me as coats and jackets were retrieved from corners, as instruments were tucked back into their cases, as the other contestants began the painful process of patching up their battered egos.

I opened up my eyes and blinked a few times until they readjusted to the glaring fluorescent lights. I saw Saul looking down at me, his expression haggard and sad.

"We lost, didn't we?" I could barely get the words out.

He nodded and helped me out of my chair.

"We didn't even get an honorable mention." This time my voice was hoarse with disbelief. I remained stunned as I slid my coat on, picked up my guitar, and followed Saul out of the Choral Room. "How could this have happened?" I was whimpering. "I was so certain that we'd win!"

"There are never any guarantees in life, Sallie," Saul said consolingly. "All there are are chances to keep on trying."

"But our song was terrific."

"So were a lot of the others." He sighed deeply and said, "I guess ours was just not the kind of thing they were looking for."

The tone of Saul's voice was flat with defeat, and so I decided to let it drop. I could see that he was in no condition to be playing straight man to my self-centered whining.

"Oh, well," I said, putting up a brave front. "You win some, you lose some. Or so they say. By the way, I'm supposed to meet Nick after he gets done here. Why don't you join us? We can all go out for ice cream or something."

"Sure." Saul shrugged. "Why not?"

I slung my arm around him, and the two of us slunk down the corridor toward the door. It had been a long evening, but I couldn't help feeling that the rest of the night was going to be even more difficult to get through.

15

"I told Nick I'd meet him at that coffee shop across the street," I told Saul as the two of us walked down the hall on our way out of the school building. I was trying to sound as cheerful as I could, trying to prevent a morose mood from taking us over and pulling us both down into the depths of despair. "He should be through with work in about fifteen minutes. I'll tell you, I could use a glass of ice cold soda or something. I'm parched. Between the hot lights while we were onstage and all the waiting around before and after . . ."

I was so busy rambling on and on, petrified by the thought of a lull in the conversation, that it wasn't until I was halfway across the street that I noticed I was alone, talking to myself like one of the many eccentrics that roam the streets of my fair city.

"Saul," I called, turning around. "Saul, where did you—?"

As I looked back at the door of the school, I could see his silhouette in the shadows as he leaned against a wall. He was talking to someone else, someone who appeared to have been waiting outside. I peered at that figure, then recognized the familiar outline, the fabric of the jacket I had seen a million times before.

"Rachel!" I screeched. "Is that really you?"

I ran back to them, my guitar banging against the side of my knees. "Did you hear us sing? Were you there, in the audience?"

"Yes, I was there," she answered softly, a sheepish look on her face. "I'm sorry you guys didn't win. But, honestly, you were terrific. Both of you."

"I can't believe you were actually there," I went on, breathless from running and from being in mild shock. "I mean, I'm thrilled, but I still can't believe it. How come you changed your mind?"

Rachel glanced at Saul before answering my question. "Well, I've been doing a lot of thinking lately, and I decided that there are some things in life that are just too good to miss out on, no matter what."

"Wow! I'm flattered!"

Honestly, sometimes I am so dense that I cannot believe it. Even though I was listening to every word Rachel was saying, I completely missed the point. I mean, I understood what she was saying about coming to our performance, but the double meaning of her statement went by me by such a long shot that I am embarrassed to admit it.

Saul, however, was so tuned in to Rachel that he knew exactly what was going on. He started to grin, and he placed his hands on her shoulders lightly.

"I'm glad to hear that you feel that way," he said, looking positively radiant. "I don't know what changed your mind, but whatever it was, I sure am glad!"

It was at that point that old banana-brain here finally caught on.

"Oh, *I* understand!" I cried all of a sudden, slapping my

forehead in an overly dramatic gesture. "You mean you've decided to reconsider your decision about seeing Saul!"

"Consider me already reconsidered." Rachel smiled. "I'm afraid that Saul is stuck with me, at least for now. Until he gets sick of me, or he starts driving me crazy with his Al Pacino imitation."

"That's great!" I put my guitar down on the sidewalk and hugged them both. "I'm so happy for both of you!" For those few minutes, I stopped feeling like someone who had just lost a very important contest, and instead felt as if I'd just won the Irish Sweepstakes. I was on top of the world. "How come you finally saw the light, Rach?"

She shrugged, and looking kind of embarrassed, she said, "I think it was partly your influence, Sallie."

"*Me*? What did I do?" I couldn't help feeling pleased.

"All your arguments finally got to me. You were right: Saul is simply too good to pass up." She kissed him on the cheek. "And I guess it just took a while for that fact to dawn on me."

"What about your parents?"

"It's not my parents' decision, it's mine. And they'll have to come to accept it, as well as the fact that from now on, I'll be making most of my own decisions. After all, in less than a year, I'll be going off to school, and I'll have to start fending for myself. Besides," she went on, pushing a strand of hair out of her eyes, "I'm the one who has to live with Rachel Glass, not them or anyone else.

"Of course, there are no guarantees. I don't know what will happen with our relationship, Saul. Neither of us can deny the fact that our backgrounds are totally different. But if we concentrate on our similarities instead of our differences, that should improve our odds right there. I can't say that I've completely resolved everything in my own mind, but I do think the important thing is that I'm going to try as hard as I can to make this work."

"I'm so glad." Saul grinned. "And you're right. Things might not work out with us, and for totally unexpected reasons. But, at least, we'll always know we gave it our best shot."

"And you'll always know that if things don't work out," I interjected, "it was because of your own personalities and differences, not because of some preconceived notions about each other."

"Sallie, is that you?" I turned to peer into the school corridor as I heard Nick's voice.

"Yes, it's me." I waved and waited for him to reach our little group. He gave me a little kiss when he joined us in the doorway.

"Sallie, Saul, you guys were terrific. Really! I can't believe you didn't win. I thought your song was the best one. Honestly."

"You have to admit that there was some pretty stiff competition up there tonight," Saul protested. "I can't say I was listening all that carefully, or all that objectively, either, but it sounded as if there were some pretty nifty tunes that we were up against."

"Well, I still think you both should be proud. This is just the beginning for the Spooner-Rodriguez songwriting team."

"Is it?" I asked dully, abruptly brought back to reality with a jolt.

"Sure," Nick insisted. "There will be lots of other opportunities."

"Name one." I had quickly relapsed into my cranky mood. I felt it was my prerogative as a temperamental artist.

"How about sending tapes of your songs to the record companies here in the city? Or singing them on Audition Night at some of the clubs down in the Village? Or even entering the contest that Alpha-Beta Records always holds in January?"

"What contest? I never heard of any Alpha-Beta contest."

"Sure, every year. It always get a big write-up in *Billboard*."

"*Billboard*? What's that?" Rachel asked.

"It's the trade magazine for the recording industry," I replied. "Who can enter it?"

"Anyone. It's for amateurs. Look, I can tell you all the details later on. The important thing is that there are opportunities all over the place. All you have to do is be willing to keep on trying. That's the key to this whole thing."

Rachel and Saul glanced at each other and smiled.

"That sounds vaguely familiar," I commented. Nick just looked blank. "Never mind, it's just an inside joke. Oh, by the way, I don't believe you two have ever been formally introduced. Nick, this is my best friend, Rachel."

"Not *the* Rachel?" His surprise was unmasked as his eyes traveled back and forth between Rachel and Saul a few times. "The Rachel the song was dedicated to?"

"*And* written for." I laughed. "One and the same."

"I'm very pleased to meet you!" Nick and Rachel shook hands. "I guess there's been a lot going on around here lately!"

"Rach, Nick and I are going out to celebrate our stellar performance tonight. Why don't you and Saul join us?"

"Sure, we'd love to," they both answered simultaneously, and all four of us broke into hysterical laughter, as if it were the funniest thing we had ever heard in our lives.

"I know a great ice cream parlor, and it's not too far away," Nick suggested. "It's called Peppermint Park."

"Oh, no!" I groaned. "My old hangout!"

"Bad choice, huh?" Poor Nick looked very confused. Between this and my reaction when he told me he was a chemistry nut, I was beginning to worry about giving the boy an inferiority complex.

"Naw, a terrific choice," I assured him. "I can take it. It'll be nice to be a customer there again. Besides, even if I did spend the best months of my life toiling away behind the take-out counter there, I can't deny the fact that they have the best hot-fudge sundaes this side of the Rockies. It's the perfect place to celebrate."

"Celebrate?" Rachel looked puzzled. "What are we celebrating?"

"You and Saul," I said.

"You and Sallie," added Saul.

"Sallie and Nick," suggested Rachel.

"The Sallie-and-Saul songwriting team." Even Nick was getting into the spirit, and he hardly knew any of us.

"And I think we should celebrate one of life's basic premises, as summed up earlier this evening by one of the world's most notable philosophers, Mr. Saul Rodriguez."

"Yes?" asked the other three in unison.

"'There are no guarantees in life, only opportunities to keep on trying.'"

"You said that, Saul?" Rachel asked dreamily. The two of them locked gazes, and even in the dim light of the streetlamp across the way, I could see that they were crazy about each other. He took her hand as we all started out for Peppermint Park. That seemed like a good idea, and so Nick and I followed their lead.

It had turned out to be a beautiful night, with a huge glowing moon that looked as if it were smiling down at us from its home high in the midnight-blue sky. The air was crisp, just cold enough to make it necessary to cuddle up next to someone special as the two of you hurried down the street, matching strides. I felt exhilarated and free, happy to be laughing and joking with three of my best friends as we made our way toward the promise of delicious ice cream, thick chocolaty sauce, and an evening of laughter and joyous closeness.

That evening seemed to capture the very essence of New York City, at least for me. The world was at peace, I was at peace, and suddenly all things seemed possible. I looked around and saw buildings that reached up to the sky, and streets that stretched on for miles and miles, and so many lights that from a distance we must have been as bright as the sun. I saw Rachel and Saul, hand in hand, flirting and giggling and just being happy together. Next to me, Nick glowed as he told me all about the Alpha-Beta songwriting contest.

I had read a poem in school once, by e.e. cummings. One of the lines that stuck in my mind for a long time was, "At that magical moment when is becomes if." I hadn't understood what it meant when I first read it, and I spent the longest time trying to figure out what it was all about. And then, as the four of us turned the corner onto First Avenue, laughing and singing against the gentle wind tinged with the icy promise of winter, I knew that I finally understood.

About the Author

CYNTHIA BLAIR grew up on Long Island, earned her B.S. from Bryn Mawr College in Pennsylvania, and went on to get a M.S. in marketing from M.I.T. She worked as a marketing manager for food companies but now has abandoned the corporate life in order to write. She lives on Long Island with her husband, Richard Smith, and their son Jesse.